FREDDIE AND THE ENORMOUS HOUSE

It was winn[...] by *Woman's R[...]* Scott to give [...] become a ful[...] ping over a [...] wrote *Freddie and t[...] [...]*, his first book, that same year [...] although it was not actually published until 1989. Since then, he has written several books, including, for Walker Books, *Why Weeps the Brogan?* (the 1989 Whitbread Children's Novel), *The Haunted Sand*, *The Camera Obscura*, *The Summertime Santa* and *Something Watching*.

Two of Hugh Scott's main interests are the supernatural and old houses, both of which play a part in Freddie – and his other books too. He lives in Helensburgh, Scotland, where, as well as writing, he draws and paints. A part-time lecturer on Creative Writing at Glasgow University, his own writing philosophy is very simple: "My only theory is that if I enjoy what I write, children may do so too."

Hugh Scott is married with two grown-up children and five cats.

08050

Also by Hugh Scott

FREDDIE AND THE ENORMOUSE

Hugh Scott

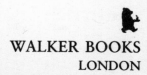

WALKER BOOKS
LONDON

First published 1989 by Walker Books Ltd
87 Vauxhall Walk, London SE11 5HJ

© 1989 Hugh Scott
Cover illustration © 1990 David Frankland

This edition published 1990

Printed in Great Britain by Cox and Wyman Ltd, Reading
Typeset in Hong Kong by Graphicraft Typesetters Ltd

British Library Cataloguing in Publication Data
Scott, Hugh
Freddie and the enormouse.
I. Title
823'.914   [J]
ISBN 0-7445-1465-7

*For
Estelle
with love*

PART ONE

1

Rain fell as thick as tears on the window of the bus. Freddie Faucet squashed his freckly nose on the glass and stared miserably at the passing countryside. All he could see were grassy hills beneath dark summer clouds, one or two cowering trees, and telephone lines looping up then down, as the bus rocked along.

Tears were not only on the window. Quite a few choked Freddie's chest and he breathed deeply to keep them down. Only a month ago his mum had died. Only a year ago his dad had been killed at work. Now he had no one.

Freddie blinked.

He tried to imagine the house he was going to live in. A grand house, someone had said, with a girl-cousin in it.

A girl.

Freddie's lower lip seemed to have a life of its own. It trembled despite his attempts to tighten it.

A girl-cousin was the last thing he wanted. He'd almost prefer to be alone, though he did feel curious about her.

Freddie couldn't remember much of what he'd been told these last few days. He knew the house was biggish and his aunt and uncle knee-deep in money, and that he had, in fact, seen them before, absolute years ago when he was a baby. But his mind was a numb confusion of memories: of his mum's smile; of her desperate letters to relatives; of a miserable four weeks he'd just spent with his father's sister — he never could bring himself to call her Aunt — and now this journey to ... he didn't know where.

The rumbling hum of the bus got into Freddie's head. He closed his eyes.

"Freddie? Freddie Faucet?"

Freddie vaguely noticed the bus had stopped and someone was pulling him to his feet.

"Little blighter's out for the count."

He dreamt he was being carried up a flight of very broad stairs and a man in armour watched till he reached the top. Then he was annoyed at being undressed like a child but everything was so far away from his mind that he couldn't protest. He only knew he was comfortable and warm.

2

Freddie lay still. He rolled his head slightly and felt a pillow under his cheek. His fingers explored a soft cover like a quilt; but no blankets. Something was worrying him. Then he remembered about his mum.

He opened his eyes.

It was darkish, yet he knew he had slept a long time. Why wasn't it morning?

He reached out cautiously and touched the velvety softness of a curtain immediately beside the bed. He struggled to his knees and pulled the curtain aside.

Daylight.

He saw a luxurious old-fashioned room. He stumbled off the bed and stared around. He gasped. He – Freddie Faucet, who had never spent a night in anything better than a single bunk-bed – had been sleeping in a four-poster!

Most of the furniture was very grand indeed. An enormous wardrobe waited patiently in the early sunlight, its wood as dark and shiny as polished chocolate. On top of a dressing-table three mirrors swung like doors and showed Freddie three other Freddies gaping at him. And lots of little drawers slid out beautifully as he investigated. The little drawers were empty, but large ones lower down held his clothes and other things from his suitcase.

A mirror stood with its back to the wall, like a detective trying not to be seen; it was twice as tall as Freddie and framed with gold flowers. At the head of the bed dangled a band of cloth, as wide as his hand, which came – very strangely – from a hole in the ceiling. The band of cloth was simply asking to be pulled, so he pulled it. He jolly well pulled it! But nothing happened. It moved a little, that was all.

Freddie examined the fireplace. It was cold to touch for it was metal, with metal flowers crawling on it and a metal mouse among the flowers. Above, hung a huge picture. It looked so heavy in its massive gold frame that Freddie reckoned it would go straight through the floor, if it fell. It was a painting of a house, or a palace. Freddie wasn't sure which. It seemed as big as Buckingham Palace, but was built of red sandstone, with ivy in the shape of monstrous hands searching along the windows.

Before the fireplace stood two chairs, one velvety and warm, with claws instead of feet, the other with lugs which hid your face when you sat back. Freddie tried them both, but couldn't decide which he liked best.

He liked the windowsill. It was broad and softly padded, and *very* cosy to sit on. Freddie could get right on to it with his back against the thickness of the wall and his legs across the width of the window.

Outside was a balcony made of fat sandstone columns all thickly wrapped in ivy, and beyond...

Freddie noticed that the window opened down the middle. He pushed it wide and clambered out, and leaned over to see gardens with stone staircases going up and down, and a lawn too big to be called a lawn rolling away towards a lake, and in the middle of the lake, on an island, amid trees and a tangle of bushes, stood ruins, the very ancient ruins, of...

"A castle!" breathed Freddie.

"*There* you are!" said a voice.

Freddie turned.

A girl was kneeling on his window seat. Her hair was shorter than Freddie's, but it wasn't reddish like his, it was fair. Her eyes were very blue and stared hard.

"I'm Lindsay Dundas," she told him. "I'm a year older than you, so you'll do what I say or I'll punch you. I'm very strong. Why did you ring the bell?"

Freddie couldn't decide whether to ask what age she was; or threaten to punch *her*; or deny even seeing a bell, never mind jolly well ringing one, so he just said, "What?"

"You pulled the bellpull." She groaned. "The thing hanging from the ceiling! It rings a bell in the kitchen! If you want breakfast, get dressed. I'll wait in the corridor."

The corridor went right and left for ever. The miles of carpet, Freddie noticed, were rather worn, but all the way along was gleaming wood and brightly coloured flowers. There wasn't a yard without a marvellous door or chair or chest or couch or table — with vases, bowls, cups, urns, statues — goodness! Freddie couldn't recognize half the things!

He followed the girl down a staircase wide enough for an army. A suit of armour was at the bottom guarding the hall. Stone pillars held up the ceiling and more suits of armour stood at doorways.

A large fireplace had its mouth filled with logs.

"Hurry up!" commanded Lindsay. "This way!"

She opened a little door and rattled down a curving stone staircase with walls you could touch easily and a cold brass rail for sliding your hand down.

They clattered into the kitchen.

The floor was stone. The fireplace was big enough to walk about in — or would have been, but for things like washing machines and cookers filling it.

The kitchen table would have filled his mum's dining room, thought Freddie, but only four places were set.

"This is Alec and Alexandra," announced Lindsay. "My parents. Alec carried you up-stairs last night. You really were flaked out. Sit down then. Help yourself to cereal. Bacon and eggs? D'you want tea, coffee, orange, grapefruit or milk? I'm having orange."

Freddie chose grapefruit. He would have preferred orange, but he wasn't having the same as this commanding girl. Imagine calling your parents by their first names! Freddie had never heard of *that!*

Alec and Alexandra were jolly nice in a distant sort of way, as if they were thinking about other things while asking how Freddie slept and telling him to feel at home as this *was* his home now, and Lindsay was glad of his company.

Lindsay said, "Hah!" quite loudly but no one told her not to be rude, and Freddie said nothing.

But he enjoyed his breakfast.

Lindsay's mother stood up and said, "Off you go now."

Freddie said, "Excuse me," and "Good-bye," to Lindsay's parents but they didn't hear, so he followed his cousin through a glass door into an outside yard surrounded by walls of the house with small windows and large shut doors big enough for horses to go through.

"Hurry up!" yelled Lindsay, and leapt away, her short hair bouncing. She ran along a low wall, balancing with her arms. Freddie hurried after her, not wanting to be outdone. The wall sloped higher and Freddie saw it went up to the roof of the building beside the yard. Lindsay ran almost all the way to the top, then clambered the last steepest part. Then she was on the roof.

She turned towards Freddie. He could tell she was judging his climbing. He ran as fast as he dared, trying not to look down. It really was pretty high. He took the steep bit cautiously.

Lindsay said, "Hmn," when he landed beside her, which Freddie thought decent, since he hadn't managed as well as she.

There were lots of peaked roofs about, like artificial hills. Lindsay led the way between them, running on wooden catwalks and narrow stone pavements. They climbed ladders and dropped from one level to another, yelling with savage delight.

Lindsay collapsed panting and howling with laughter beside a chimneystack.

"Pretty good for a little blighter!" she gasped as Freddie fell beside her.

He didn't have enough breath to object at her calling him little. He didn't mind being called a blighter, though. In fact, he rather enjoyed it.

"How high are we?" asked Freddie, when he recovered. He couldn't see the ground for roofs.

"Only two storeys. But we're going higher if you've the nerve."

Lindsay's blue eyes stared hard at him.

Freddie was suddenly conscious of the freckles on his nose. He looked away.

"Sure," he said.

Then she was off, lean as a monkey, leaping down walls, clambering over tiled mountains, and once, edging dangerously round a giant chimneystack, her face towards a very long drop into a dark space between buildings.

Freddie's nerve nearly gave out and he was glad he had on shoes with gripping soles. But he managed, and smiled at her as he stepped to safety. She smiled back by pulling her mouth down, then she darted away.

Then she stopped.

3

Before them towered a red sandstone wall as tall as a cliff. Fastened to its dizzy surface was a thin iron ladder.

"That goes to the main part of the house," said Lindsay, watching him carefully. "Super view up there." She stood still, her blue eyes judging him, her hair shifting slightly in the breeze.

Freddie tried not to show concern.

"Are you allowed up there? My mum wouldn't let..." He stared up trying not to think of his mum, but the wind seemed to make his eyes water.

"I don't mind," shrugged Lindsay. "We'll go this way." And she darted along the foot of the great wall, along catwalks and funny little paths, around skylights and chimneys — some of stone, some of brick, some of metal — and once she strode across a gap without any hesitation at all, and Freddie went to do likewise but stepped back, for beneath him was nothing but a dark slit.

"It's not wide," said Lindsay.

It wasn't wide. It was an easy step — or would have been but for the awful feeling of darkness, and a dreadful, narrow place to fall into.

Freddie jumped.

He cleared it with lots to spare and managed a smile to himself, though he hoped there was an easier way to the ground.

They stopped beside a circular brick chimney which looked very old. They had a view from the back of the house. Fields and paddocks and trees were spread out below like patches of coloured cloth. Beyond were gentle hills and, hiding in valleys, a village and a distant town.

Freddie was going to ask which town it was when a strange deep sound rumbled gently all around.

He looked about in surprise.

Where could it be coming from?

And what could possibly cause such a roaring and grumbling, such a snuffling, mumbling jumble of noise in this quiet countryside? Then he realized.

It was coming from the old brick chimney!

He looked at Lindsay to ask her about the noise, but only got as far as opening his mouth and positioning his tongue for the first word when he saw that her eyes were wide open so he could see the whites all round the blue pupils, and her face was pale as if she were sick.

So he changed his question, and said instead, "What's wrong? Are you ill?"

"We've got to go," she said, and went.

"But what is it? What's that noise?"

"Nothing. I want a drink."

He followed her as she dropped from one roof to the next. The last drop to the ground was very high.

"Bet y'can't do this one," challenged Lindsay.

She went to the very edge and, to Freddie's amazement, held on to the stone gutter and lowered herself over. It was a long way down.

"You can't!" said Freddie.

"Bet?"

"Don't!" He could only see the top of her head and her eyes like blue searchlights.

"I've done it before."

"Come up!"

"You scared?"

"It's too high!"

"Only for boys with freckles." She let go. Freddie gasped.

The ground below was grassy and sloped steeply away from the building. Lindsay landed on her feet and fell on to her side, then rolled face-up, face-away down the slope. She lay panting.

"There!" She got on to her knees. "I win the bet!"

Freddie looked over in dismay. He could never jump that. "How do I get down?" he shouted, feeling slightly desperate now he was alone on the rooftop landscape.

"Oh, go that way!" said Lindsay. "The

wall comes right to the ground in steps. Watch the gargoyle doesn't bite you!"

Freddie patted the stone monster's head. He saw it was really a drain to send water from the gutter through its mouth away from the wall, but it looked very fierce like a strange human crouching on the edge of the building with heavy folded wings and a dreadful head. If it stood up it would be taller than Lindsay.

He stopped patting it and was relieved to clamber down the stepped wall and have a normal looking-across view of everything. When he thought about his climb down the wall later, he marvelled at how easily he'd done it. After seeing the crazy drop Lindsay had made, the wall was nothing. But he would never have done it on his own.

Lindsay Dundas, thought Freddie, was the craziest person he'd ever met. He liked her more than he would admit.

They strolled round lots of corners and through a door and endless rooms and corridors and popped into the kitchen. They had a drink and tried to decide whose face was the dirtier. Lindsay won that too, because she had rolled down the grassy slope.

"But what was that noise?" asked Freddie.

"The wind in the chimney. Bet you can't guess how many bathrooms we've got!"

"Four!"

"No!"

"Five?"

"Cold."

"Two."

"Colder."

"Six?" gasped Freddie.

"Freezing!"

"A thousand!"

"No! Don't be a twerp!"

"Ten."

"Give in?"

"Eleven," guessed Freddie.

"Fourteen."

"Fourteen!"

"Or fifteen, or sixteen. They're scattered all over, some in the bedrooms. I always lose count."

"Sixteen!"

"Nobody knows how many rooms. Well over a hundred."

"A *hundred!* Our house only had four! That's like twenty-five houses! It's a whole street!"

"More," said Lindsay, "and dozens more still in the cellars."

"Cellars! Golly!"

"But we can't go down there. Let's raid the fridge. I'm starving!"

So they had a snack of cold boiled ham and pickles and cottage cheese and butter and tomato and some green things Freddie didn't recognize and didn't like to ask what they were. What a first day!

The afternoon vanished in a haze of excitement.

Then, when the castle's reflection lay dark on the lake and the sun slid reluctantly from the sky, Freddie had a bath in one of the sixteen bathrooms. It was through a secret door in his own room – well, an almost secret door – hidden behind the big mirror which swung out magically and there was his very own private bathroom!

He thought he would lie awake half the night thinking of rooftops and jumping and climbing and Lindsay rolling on the grass, but once he had clambered into his amazing four-poster bed and pulled the curtains cosily round, he remembered absolutely nothing.

The next thing he knew was light in his eyes and Lindsay in jeans and a sweatshirt, bouncing on the bed and yelling rude things to make him get up.

He wasn't used to girls, especially in his room, so he insisted on being alone to dress, but he was very curious, and anxious, when Lindsay said, "Well, hurry up, because I've got horrible news for you."

He hurried, but had to dig out a change of clothes from the long drawer in the dressing-table because yesterday's clothes had vanished. He stared at the three anxious Freddies in the mirrors.

"I don't want to leave," he whispered to them. "I don't want to leave!"

4

"Come on!" yelled Lindsay through the door.

Freddie pulled on his good-grip shoes and went into the corridor. "What's wrong?" he asked, desperate to know the worst. "Do I have to leave? I don't have to go to an orphanage?"

"You are an ass!" said Lindsay. "Alec told you yesterday — this is your home. You'll never have to leave!"

"Never?"

"Never, never! Now listen!"

Freddie was so relieved that he didn't hear Lindsay's first words.

". . . coming today. She's the most foul creature. . ."

"Who?"

"I've just told you! Don't boys ever listen? Anaglypta. She's my cousin — and I suppose yours too in a way. She's an absolute dirty toenail! She stuffs herself with grub, wears the most awful clothes, she's a fat horrible worm and I was in trouble most of last summer because of her."

"Why is she coming?"

"Her father's got business abroad so she's coming here since it's the school hols. She normally goes to boarding school. *He* can't stand her either. So *we* have to suffer."

"We can keep out her way."

"We have to look after her. We're the hosts..."

"We?"

"You and me."

Freddie felt something like excitement and bursting joy billowing inside him. *He* was host in this marvellous house! He wanted to hug Lindsay but she went on talking — not that he would have.

"She follows you about. I couldn't go anywhere last time. She'd even be outside the loo waiting for me! There's the breakfast gong!"

They fled down the stairs, and Freddie saluted the suits of armour.

After breakfast, despite Lindsay's groans, they went by car to the station which was at the town Freddie had seen from the roof. They waited at the barrier. When the train arrived Lindsay's father instructed them to watch for Anaglypta.

"Look for the widest one," hissed Lindsay as the train broke open and spilled its contents on to the platform.

Freddie saw quite a few wide people, but they were grown up.

"There!" groaned Lindsay. "Oh, Alec," she told her father, "she's fatter than ever! Did you padlock the fridges? Look at that!"

The three of them stared.

Plodding slowly in the midst of the rush

was a large pink blob with a smaller pink blob — cousin Anaglypta's head — on top. Trailing from her tiny hands were two suitcases on wheels. She caught sight of Lindsay and stopped, letting the cases bump down. She waved at them to come and help.

Lindsay hung over the barrier and grinned, shaking her head. "We're not allowed in!" she yelled. "I don't believe it!" she added. "No one's as fat as that! She looks as if she's swallowed a pig! Come to think of it, she looks like a pig!"

Alec murmured something, but Lindsay only gave him a little glance. "Come on, Anaglypta! You can do it! Whee!"

Freddie looked at Lindsay in surprise. She seemed pleased to see Anaglypta.

"I thought you didn't like her," he whispered.

"But I've just thought," said Lindsay. "There are two of us now, and only one Anaglypta — or has she got friends under that awful pink tent she's wearing! She'll still be a pain in the saddle, but I have you. Maybe it won't be so bad. Can you see her," she whispered, as Anaglypta reached the barrier and dug out her ticket, "climbing over the roof?"

Anaglypta stood puffing and scowling.

"I needed help," she complained.

She had blue eyes, but unlike Lindsay's they were all closed up with fat and constant scowling. Her little pink mouth opened and shut like a goldfish as she gasped in air.

Alec carried the cases and Lindsay stared at Anaglypta's bulk as she waddled along, complaining about absolutely everything.

Freddie was glad when the long drive was over. Anaglypta had been very hot and smelled rather, of soap and perfume. Lindsay hadn't said anything, but opened the car window and grinned secretly to herself.

It was lunchtime when they arrived home. Anaglypta would have sat down at the table immediately but scowled at Alexandra's suggestion that she would feel better after a bath and change of clothes.

When Anaglypta reappeared, Lindsay had difficulty in not shrieking with laughter. Freddie could see it bubbling inside her. Even her parents looked at each other the way grownups do, and talked about other things. Anaglypta had somehow forced her lower half into a pair of the biggest jeans Freddie had ever seen. She wore a yellow shirt with short sleeves which bit into her arms like knotted wire. Her hair, Freddie noticed, was red – not dark red like his – but an orange frizz.

Anaglypta was seated first. She devoured everything within arm's length and paid no attention to anything else. She didn't hear Lindsay's remarks about certain foods being fattening, and didn't notice Alec's quiet smile nor Alexandra's hints that perhaps she should eat a little less quickly. Everything those tiny fat hands could reach disappeared into the pink mouth.

At last Anaglypta sat back groaning. Alexandra shooed them away gently and Freddie followed Lindsay through the glass door into the courtyard. Anaglypta lumbered at his back. "I want to explore the house!" she complained. "I didn't see it all last time. I don't want to go out! I want to see the cellars and the swimming pool and the dining hall where a hundred people can sit at the table, and go up the towers and..." She had run out of breath.

Lindsay looked at Freddie with a question in her blue eyes.

"I wouldn't mind seeing the house," said Freddie.

"We'll go round to the West Door and I'll introduce you to the peacocks," said Lindsay. "Race you!"

"Peacocks!" gasped Freddie, and he ran after her, ignoring Anaglypta's, "I'm too tired to run! Wait, you beasts!"

"Too fat, she means," said Lindsay when she let Freddie catch up.

They went through a great stone archway. The keystone grinned down on them with its carved animal head. They were through the arch before Freddie recognized what the carving represented, for it was worn with centuries of rain and wind.

"A mouse!" said Freddie, and stopped so suddenly that Lindsay was half a dozen paces ahead before she could turn.

"Where?" she demanded anxiously.

It was the first time Freddie had seen something like fear in this daredevil cousin.

"The carved head on the archway." He turned and saw another mouse's head on the side of the arch facing him. "There's another. It's not so worn."

"Oh, is that all? That one's sheltered from the weather."

They wandered on, waiting for the wobbling Anaglypta to catch up.

"But why mouse carvings?" asked Freddie. "Why not something grand like a lion or unicorn or a bear? They have bears all over the place in Warwickshire."

"I don't know. Hurry up, Anaglypta! Is she really as fat as that! *I'm* jolly well *never* going to get fat!"

The sky was clearing above the trees. The sun touched them with warm fingers and they found a grassy place to sit; and while Lindsay chatted and Anaglypta lay flat on her back with her little mouth opening and shutting, Freddie sat with a smile relaxing his face and his thoughts flickering from rooftop mountains to four-poster beds, then to soft curving hills, and mouse-heads and the strange growling sound of the wind in the old chimney.

"Where does that chimney come from?" he asked suddenly.

"Which?" said Lindsay, frowning hard as she pulled up grass stalks and tied them into knots.

"The one the noise came out."

"Oh, an old furnace in the cellar. Part of the heating system."

"I want to see it," said Anaglypta.

"Well you can't! It's blocked off. Nobody goes down there but Alec and men who repair things."

"I want to! You're supposed to be entertaining me! I'm the guest remember! Just because you two live here you don't need to be mean about your cellar! It's not a secret! Is that where you keep your money? My father says you lot are loaded. If you don't take me I'll tell Uncle Alec and he'll give you the most awful row!"

Anaglypta pushed herself up and stood with her little fists where her waist should have been, and thrust out her elbows angrily. "You take me to the cellar, then I want something to drink and a sandwich. And don't try to run off without me — I know where the West Door is!"

"Oh, do shut up!" said Lindsay. "Come on, Freddie!"

Outside the West Door were lawns, rather whiskery at the edges, and rose gardens perfuming the summer air, and hedges, straggling a little, but with lumps here and there in shapes of birds and animals.

"That's called topiary," Lindsay told Freddie. "There's a peacock..."

"I thought you meant real peacocks," said Freddie, a shade disappointed, though the hedge peacocks were really quite marvellous.

"What d'you think *that* is," said Lindsay, pointing along the path.

Sailing towards them was the most beautiful and simply grandest bird Freddie had ever seen. It shimmered with metallic colours of green and blue and had a strange little plume decorating its head. Its tail swept the ground like a king's robe.

"Golly!" he said.

"There are more," said Lindsay.

"Do they wander where they like?"

"Oh, yes, but they're well looked after. You'll see plenty of people around. We don't run this place on our own, y'know. Though Alec wishes we could afford another gardener."

Freddie stared and stared. He looked at the hedge-peacock and thought how cleverly it was made. Then he noticed the mouse. A hedge mouse!

"There's more mouse!" he exclaimed.

"Mice must have something to do with the history of this place. Maybe it was over-run at one time and an army of cats was brought in..."

"Anaglypta!" yelled Lindsay. "Don't touch the peacock! You can't eat it, you gannet! Let's go in! You want to see the cellar, don't you?"

"I'd rather see the kitchen," moaned Anaglypta.

"You've just finished lunch!"

"That was only a snack," said Anaglypta contemptuously.

"You had as much as Freddie and I together. *And* the parents, *and* the peacocks, *and*..."

"Shut up, you beast!" Anaglypta's orange frizz vibrated with indignation and tears squeezed from her eyes. She immediately rubbed her hands across her cheeks, leaving her face streaked with dirt.

"Oh, stop blubbing!" said Lindsay. "I was only teasing. What d'you want to eat? An elephant's leg sandwich?"

Anaglypta wailed and lumbered through the West Door.

"She'll blab to Alec," said Lindsay. "We'd better console her. The parents take this host-and-guest thing seriously. We don't want to be confined to the playrooms with her!"

Freddie hadn't seen the playrooms. There

was so much! He grinned to himself. Everything was so exciting! He wondered if he could ever get to know all about this wonderful house.

They ran into the entrance hall. It wasn't quite as large as the other hall, but it had suits of armour, great patterns of swords and old pistols fanned out on the walls and two gigantic fireplaces. Anaglypta was sitting on the bottom step of the staircase, forcing herself to sob. The fat on her pink arms wobbled like strawberry jelly.

"Come on, Anaglypta," said Lindsay fairly gently. "We'll take you to the kitchen."

"I'm not hungry!"

"You said you were!"

"I want to see the cellar!"

"You said you were hungry!"

"I want..."

Freddie wasn't interested in cousin Anaglypta's wants. It seemed to him she started every sentence with I want. He wandered about looking at the weapons, wondering what it would be like wearing a suit of armour to school.

He stared with his mouth open at one of the fireplaces. It was rather dusty, but magnificent, built of stone, with columns like a town hall, and a mantlepiece higher than Freddie could reach and alive with sculptured flowers and animals. In the middle, above the fireplace opening, was carved a mouse and a man. The man was trying to kill the mouse with a sword, because the mouse was bigger — much bigger — than he was.

Then...

As Freddie stood staring...

As Anaglypta complained...

As Lindsay argued...

From the fireplace surged a roaring and grumbling, such a snuffling, mumbling jumble of noise...!

5

Lumps of soot plopped into the grate. Freddie stepped back in surprise and looked at Lindsay.

She was standing very still, her eyes wide. Anaglypta was sniffling, but watching Lindsay through her tears.

"Wow!" said Freddie. "I didn't know there *was* a wind blowing! Lindsay, what's the matter?"

For long seconds Lindsay just stared at the fireplace, her eyes getting wider and wider, then...

She walked off, as if trying not to run.

Freddie went after her but didn't say anything. He couldn't understand girls. This one was so daring, and said things he wouldn't dream of saying, and yet she was scared of wind in the chimneys. But he didn't like to see her upset.

"I wouldn't mind some orange juice," he said.

"All right," said Lindsay, not really sounding like herself.

Maybe, thought Freddie, she was angry with Anaglypta. That was it. Anaglypta had said something to hurt her. Lindsay Dundas was never frightened of a noise! No chance! Freddie decided he would take some responsibility for Anaglypta, after all – and a large grin pushed his cheeks out – he was the host too! He would give Anaglypta a telling off, so he said to Lindsay, "What did she say?"

"Who?"

"Anaglypta, of course. What did she say to annoy you?"

"Everything she says annoys me."

"But you went all pale."

"I didn't!"

"You did!"

"No, I didn't!" She stopped and blazed at him with her terrible gaze. "Don't you say I turned pale! I'm not scared of anything! I can climb higher than you, Freddie Faucet, and jump bigger jumps! And I bet I can ride faster and swim faster too! Don't you dare say I'm scared!"

She whirled away and stood in front of one of the heavy gold-framed paintings which hung every few yards in the rooms and corridors.

Anaglypta was trudging towards them, her face still streaked with tears, but scowling instead of crying.

Freddie was trying to understand Lindsay. He hadn't *said* she was scared, just pale, and he was even more bewildered when she turned on him, grabbed him by the arm and said in a voice he recognized, "Let's see how much Anaglypta can eat before she bursts like a balloon. If we stick a pin in her she'll frizzle away into a little bit of pink skin!"

Freddie grinned delightedly. This was Lindsay talking!

Lindsay interrupted Anaglypta's stream of I wants with, "We're *going* to the kitchen! And you can have anything you choose!"

In the kitchen, they sat Anaglypta at the table, Lindsay guiding her into the strongest chair and smiling wickedly at Freddie. Freddie joined in her game and they served the astonished Anaglypta with orange juice to start, and while she gulped that they sliced a pile of bread and shovelled on cheese and pickle and meat, drowned it in mayonnaise and carried it to the table on a gigantic blue and white oval plate.

"For you, Angalypta," said Lindsay the hostess. "Would you care for some milk now? Milk for Anaglypta, Frederick. Not that fridge! The one in the fireplace!"

They watched fascinated as Anaglypta, with great pride, munched her way through the whole plate of sandwiches and drank tidal waves of milk. When she finished, she smiled. Freddie had thought that Anaglypta might be quite pretty if she smiled but he liked her smile even less than her scowl. It was so smug, so self-satisfied. He shook his head. How could anyone so absolutely bloated be satisfied with herself!

Anaglypta's smile wavered. Her pink face lost its pinkness and grew greenish.

Very politely, Lindsay, with a regal tilt of her head, indicated one of the many doors out of the kitchen. "The nearest loo," she murmured, "is through there, first on the right."

Anaglypta said, "Ooh!" and lurched away, her arms across her bulging front.

The door swung shut behind her and Lindsay howled. "We did it!" she yelled. "We burst Anaglypta! We'll tell *The Guinness Book of Records!*" She pretended to write a letter. "Dear Mr Guinness, on this day at 2.15 Greenwich Mean Time, Miss Lindsay Dundas and Mr Freddie Faucet succeeded in exploding the incredible elastic schoolgirl, Anaglypta, signed, L.D. and F.F. Whee!"

And they laughed until tears came. Then they made themselves a reasonable snack and enjoyed each other's company very much indeed.

"What d'you want to do now?" asked Lindsay.

"Well, I'd like to see..." Freddie thought of the dining room Anaglypta had mentioned that could seat a hundred people. He thought of the swimming pool, the cellars, the fields — why, he hadn't even seen the main part of the house except for his own room!

"The castle! Can we see the castle?"

Lindsay smiled by pulling her mouth down,

which Freddie found curious, but nice.

"Out of bounds, Freckles," she said. "D'you always choose the wrong thing?" she asked, and punched his shoulder. "I've only been in it once. It's dangerous and not very interesting."

Freddie thought it couldn't be any more dangerous than running like mad about the rooftops, but he didn't say so.

Lindsay told him. "Bits of walls keep falling down. It's really jolly ancient. Sometimes you hear a splash in the lake and there goes another stone. It's not worth visiting and the parents are pretty sticky about it. They don't bother about most things but the castle is definitely *out* – like the deepest cellars and being beastly to guests. I wonder where Anaglypta is. She can't have fallen down the loo – even we don't have one *that* big!"

They went after Anaglypta. Lindsay knocked on the door.

"Are you all right?" she asked loudly.

The key clunked in the lock, and Anaglypta's ginger frizz appeared, with her face under it as pale and round as the moon, except for the dirty streaks.

"You look foul," said Lindsay cheerfully. "Why don't you heave off to bed? You'll feel better by dinner time."

"Oh, shut up! I'll never eat again!" Anaglypta pushed past them and drifted slowly along the passageway, looking, as Lindsay said, like a balloon with jeans and shirt painted on it. Freddie thought she wasn't that bad.

Then Lindsay said, "Whee!" to Freddie without actually making any sound, and he smiled back at her and this time *he* punched *her* arm, very gently.

"Free!" whispered Lindsay and they fled back through the kitchen, out the glass door and into the sunshine.

The sky stretched blue for a million miles. They ran along an earthy road, slipped through a wire fence, across a paddock and darted among trees.

Lindsay seemed suddenly to decide where they were going and changed direction slightly. Freddie followed close at her heels. He liked the way the sunlight spilled through the trees, splintering into lines of light, making friendly bright places and mysterious shadowy corners. Lindsay stopped and he ran into her, and they fell tumbling and shrieking with laughter on the warm grass and moss.

"My tree!" gasped Lindsay pointing upwards. "It's the best tree in the world for climbing and once you're up, no one can see you. It's a great place to be alone. You're the only person I've told about it." She looked at Freddie solemnly. "Swear you won't tell. Not even Alec and Alexandra."

"I swear," said Freddie, and he felt very proud and suddenly very secure as a member of this, *his* family.

"Race you to the house!" cried Lindsay.

Freddie scrambled up but was startled to see Lindsay, not dashing the way they had come, but throwing herself tummy-first over a low branch of the tree. In a second she was standing on the branch, reaching up among the leaves then, with a wriggle, her denim legs swung upwards and disappeared.

Freddie didn't stop to wonder why she had challenged him to race home then shot into the tree — he too was tummy-first over the branch and hauling himself after her, and in moments he was a jungle creature, supple and strong trailing his prey though the leafy green world.

"Well done!" cried Lindsay.

Freddie said, "Wow!" in admiration, for Lindsay was sitting on a platform of branches, which had walls of branches, which had a roof of branches!

So this was the house she was racing to!

"Come on in!" said Lindsay. There was just room for him. "I left a window so I could see out."

"Did you build this yourself?" gasped Freddie.

"Of course! I told you no one knows about it! And you'd better not tell!"

"I promised, didn't I?"

He looked through the window. The real house was quite a distance away. It was as long as a street and built of red sandstone, with giant ivy hands clinging to the walls.

"It's the house in the picture!" he said. "Above the fireplace in my room. It's as big as Buckingham Palace!"

"Pretty nearly," said Lindsay.

"And I can see the lake and the castle. I can see the castle more clearly..."

Freddie's blood tingled coldly. All the joyfulness of this summer's day drained out of him. He knew his face had gone white like paper.

He knew his fingers were gripping the branches of the wall so tightly that his knuckles were sore.

But he couldn't move.

He couldn't speak.

He could scarcely even breathe!

6

"What is it?" demanded Lindsay.

Freddie just stared towards the castle, his blood as cold as ice-cream.

"What d'you see!" screamed Lindsay, and pushed him aside. She looked sharply at the lake, then turned on Freddie.

"What did you see!" she shouted. "Tell me! Tell me this instant! If you don't speak I'll throw you out this tree and break all your bones! Freddie Faucet!"

Freddie didn't know what he had seen. He knew he'd seen the lake, still as a mirror, blue as the sky, showing him upside-down trees and upside-down ruins of the castle. Then he'd seen a movement among the reflected stones and thought it was a fish or duck in the water.

Then he'd realized the movement was not in the water at all, but in the real ruins which were not quite hidden by trees and tangles of bushes.

Then he'd seen a heavy stone from the top of the ancient wall topple and clatter silently in the distance, down the sloping ground, crushing bushes and reeds and hitting the water in a soundless splash.

He *thought* he heard the crashing and splash a few seconds later and *thought* he saw

... No! He *did* see an enormous curved back just showing as it moved among the ruins! A tremendous animal shape, so fantastic it almost stopped his breathing! It was huge! It was grey. It could only be...

"An elephant?" said Freddie.

"An elephant!" yelled Lindsay. "Don't be such a prune! How could an elephant be in the lake!"

"In the castle," he said doubtfully.

She stared so hard at Freddie he thought her blue eyes would freeze him into a block of ice. Then she turned sharply and watched the island for a long time.

"It must have been a bird," she said at last. "Owls live there. You saw one of them flitting about. You *are* an ass, Freckles!"

"Owls in the daytime?" said Freddie.

"Of course, owls in the daytime! I've seen them often! They're not chained up because it's daylight, y'know! Did you see a whole elephant?" she challenged. "Trunk? Legs? Ears? Well?"

"Just its back."

"Just its back!" snorted Lindsay. "Moving through the ruins. Or an owl or a dove or a duck, or even a rabbit on the ground, or a squirrel on the wall..."

"I thought I saw a curved grey back!" said Freddie. He was wondering what he did see. Lindsay was right — how could it be an elephant? He supposed it might have been a squirrel moving on the wall and giving an impression of... He smiled at Lindsay, and shrugged. He didn't know what to say because he didn't know what to think.

"I'll bet it was Anaglypta!" declared Lindsay. "She was sleeping, rolled off her bed, bounced out the window, trundled down the lawn, splashed into the lake and was shipwrecked on the island! Only it couldn't have been her cos she's *bigger* than an elephant!"

And they howled with laughter and relief.

They talked for hours.

They peered through the window at the lake.

They planned to extend the tree house and thought up a way of building a fireplace so that they could have picnics with cooked food. Then with the summer sun warming their sleepy faces, they decided it was time to go.

"A bath before dinner," commanded Lindsay quietly. "Dinner's in the Great Hall."

That aroused Freddie from his dozy warm feeling. Up to that second – as they wandered through the scented woods... As they strolled up the earthy road and in the glass door of the kitchen... As they climbed the stone staircase and the main staircase... As he turned the brass handle of his bedroom door – up to that second he didn't know whether he was hungrier than he was sleepy, or sleepier than he was hungry. But the Great Hall!

"Where a hundred people can sit round one table?" he gasped, his eyes wide awake.

"More or less!" said Lindsay. "Hurry up! The gong will be going soon. I'll come and get you!"

The Great Hall!

Wow!

7

Freddie found clothes laid out on his bed. The curtains round the bed were nicely drawn back and looped to the four posts by being tucked into brass rings. Everything was so grand!

Freddie had never seen the clothes before. They weren't his.

Or were they?

He reckoned they were!

There was a white shirt with ruffles down the front and a bow-tie the colour of a plum. He felt the shirt. It was softer and shinier than anything he'd ever seen. He wondered if it was maybe a bit girlish.

There was a pair of black satiny trousers with a curiously-shaped velvet band lying across them. The band was the same plum colour as the tie. On the floor were shoes that shone like black glass. Tucked into one shoe was a new pair of socks, also black and with a tiny pattern up the outside. He looked closely at the pattern. It was a row of tiny mouse heads. Freddie grinned, and thought how marvellous everything was. How terrific to be living in this amazing house. How super to have new things without having to ask his mum a hundred times...

He turned away from the bed and saw the

three Freddies who lived in the mirrors looking at him sadly. He would give up all this to have his mum and dad back. His eyes were hot and his lower lip trembled. He hauled open the secret door and rushed into the bathroom.

To his astonishment the bath was full of steaming water, and soap and towels waited for him. He forgot his lower lip and in no time at all was up to his ears in bubbles. Then he was pulling on the new clothes, and the three Freddies looked very proud, and they bowed to him as he bowed to them.

He was just brushing his hair when Lindsay knocked and came in. Freddie turned.

And gasped.

And gaped.

Lindsay Dundas, the tomboy with the short hair, jeans and sweatshirt, had been replaced by a Lindsay Dundas with ankles, a blue dress that glittered in the evening light and a mass of fair hair piled elegantly on her head.

And she was wearing make-up.

"How did you do that!" cried Freddie, not really sure if this new creature *was* Lindsay.

Lindsay smiled her pulled-down smile and admired herself in the big mirror on the secret door.

"It's nothing," she said casually, and sailed out.

Freddie dived after her. He reached up to

her hair. "Where did all that come from?"

"Don't touch! You shouldn't ask a lady how she works her magic. You just tell her she's charming!"

"But where did it come from?"

"It's a hairpiece, idiot! I pin it on! And where's your cummerbund? Why aren't you wearing it?"

She pushed Freddie back into his room and put the plum-coloured velvet band around his waist and clipped it at his back. "*That's* a cummerbund!" she told him. "Now let's see what Anaglypta's doing!"

They walked along the corridor away from the staircase.

"That's my suite next to yours," said Lindsay.

"Suite?"

"Suite of rooms! Don't you know anything! We've both got a bedroom, a bathroom, a dressing room and a sitting room."

"I haven't got all that!"

"You just haven't noticed. I'll show you later. Anaglypta's next again." She knocked on the door.

There was no reply, so she turned the handle and marched in, Freddie drifting behind in her cloud of perfume. He wished he knew what a hairpiece was.

Anaglypta was flat on her back on the bed. Not, noticed Freddie, with satisfaction, a four-poster — though the room was just as grand as his.

"She's the great pink whale," said Lindsay.

Anaglypta lay like a jelly in clothes, as dirty as ever, snoring and grunting, her little tongue vibrating on her lower lip.

"What a sight! Get up, Anaglypta! Dinner time!"

Anaglypta struggled awake and quivered all over as she stretched. She got up and pushed past Lindsay heading for the door.

"Bath!" yelled Lindsay.

"I don't need a bath!" squealed Anaglypta.

"You jolly well do! If you think you're sitting in the Great Hall looking like that you'd better think again! We're dressed, and Alec and Alexandra will be dressed. They don't mind you looking like a bag of dirty laundry in the kitchen — but not tonight! Now get into your bath! It's probably half cold by now. Hard luck! Go! Go!"

Anaglypta scowled, but went.

"The gong will sound in five minutes!" yelled Lindsay through the door.

They waited in the corridor, sitting together on one gigantic wooden chair carved into a confusion of things which were wonderful to touch. All the chairs and chests and benches and clocks and what-nots along the endless corridor shone with age and pride. There were vases on every flat surface, many with fresh flowers, and paintings and mirrors and maps in frames.

It was breathtaking!

Anaglypta appeared.

"Why does she always wear bright pink?" hissed Lindsay. "Not blue shoes, Anaglypta!"

Anaglypta peered over her stomach at her feet. "I know that!" she said, and went back into her room.

She reappeared with pink shoes and a smear of lipstick partly on her lips and partly on her cheek.

"That will do, I suppose," sighed Lindsay. "Now hurry up! The gong went ages ago."

They didn't go down the main stair, but past it, continuing along the corridor. Lindsay stopped at a very large pair of doors. She pushed them open and walked in.

Well. It wouldn't have seated a hundred people. And the table was old. Old and worn, saw Freddie, but really, he supposed, quite magnificent. And it had so many legs, with so many grand chairs around, that he couldn't count them all. And the bulbous parts of the legs were carved, looking like strange knobbly knees, and the table top was carved around the edge. He saw that the wood had been polished affectionately over the centuries and the more he looked, the more he liked this furniture and this beautiful room, with ancient sideboards which Lindsay said were court cupboards.

"It used to seat a hundred," she whispered, "when there were two tables. Grandfather Dundas lost one in a bet."

"Oh," said Freddie, and he peered at the five places set for dinner.

His mouth opened. The knives and forks and spoons were made of gold.

Anaglypta was already seated, gold cutlery in her fists, looking at the court cupboards where food was simmering on hotplates waiting to be served.

A whole marvellous wall of windows looked out over the lawn and lake and distant summer countryside.

Lindsay prodded Anaglypta until she stood up, then Alec and Alexandra — who had been seated at the windows sipping drinks — came to the table and sat down. Only then did Lindsay let Anaglypta sit. Freddie and Lindsay and Anaglypta were facing the view outside.

Then came the food.

Oh, it was good! Freddie had never smelled such smells, tasted such tastes or seen such astonishing things to eat. He ate almost as much as Anaglypta. He ate more than Lindsay. And he was full, full, full!

Then...

Oh, then...

8

Freddie was leaning back in his great chair. If he could have loosened his cummerbund he would. His eyes took in the trees around the lake. He admired the water which looked as if an artist had dipped a red brush in it; he saw the ruins of the castle through the trees and the flattened bushes and grass where the large stone had crashed down, and...

Oh, golly.

Freddie knew his face had gone as white as paper – again. He knew his fingers were gripping the arms of his chair so tightly that his knuckles hurt – again. But he couldn't move, or speak or scarcely even breathe – again.

Then he breathed very carefully.

He glanced at Lindsay. She hadn't noticed anything. She was chattering to her parents who, of course, had their backs to the window. Angalypta was devouring an orange. Freddie looked at the island.

He saw nothing unusual. He thought carefully. Last time, he'd seen an elephant that couldn't have been an elephant. This time . . .

He decided to ask.

"Uncle Alec," he said quietly, trying not to show his excitement, "are there any snakes here?"

"Snakes, Freddie? Plenty of grass snakes and slow worms. An adder or two – watch out for them y'know. Have you seen any?"

"I just wondered if – " Freddie avoided the question – "if there are any really big snakes. Brown ones." He looked away from his uncle's blue eyes which stared at him the way Lindsay's did. Alec took a cigar from a gold box, snipped the end with a gold cutter and lit it with a gold lighter which he held in both hands. Blue smoke clouded his face.

He said, "No," and his gaze became vague. Freddie breathed out.

"May we be excused?" said Lindsay suddenly.

"Off you go," said Alec. "Did you enjoy your meal?"

Freddie said, "Thank you," four or five times, and with Lindsay hauling Anaglypta, they left the Great Hall.

"What's going on?" demanded Lindsay once they were in the corridor. "Why did you ask about snakes? We haven't seen any!"

Anaglypta wandered off gazing at the paintings.

"You won't believe me," said Freddie, trying to keep his eyes on Lindsay's.

"Tell me, or I'll empty your dinner out of you!"

He told her. He had just relaxed back into his chair and was admiring the red sunlight on the lake, when he saw. . . When he saw. . .

It was in the grass and partly in water. It was long and grey-brown, and curved among the ruins. He didn't see its head. It was so long, he told Lindsay, that if it were in his room it would stretch the whole length of his bed, across the width of it, and along the whole length again!

"Bosh!" said Lindsay.

"I said you wouldn't believe me!"

"You're not a liar, are you, Freddie Faucet? I couldn't stand having a liar in the house! *Liars can't be trusted!*" Her eyes stared into him dreadfully. Freddie felt his face blushing. This time he returned Lindsay's stare.

"I am not a liar," he said quietly. They continued to look at each other. "If you don't believe me," said Freddie, "we'll go to the island and see properly!"

Lindsay said nothing.

"I saw a snake!" he insisted.

"And an elephant!" muttered Lindsay scornfully, but Freddie thought her eyes were unsure, as if she suspected something.

"All right," she said, "we'll *go* to the island – *tomorrow!*"

9

The water was cool on Freddie's feet and legs. The mud squelched deliciously between his toes. Then the mud was too deep and gripped his feet like a sucking mouth. He plunged forwards and swam.

Lindsay was swimming quietly ahead of him towards the island. Freddie found he could catch up easily and he pulled himself over the grassy bank before she reached it. He didn't look at her but could feel her surprise at being beaten. She stood beside him.

The sun was warm on their dripping bodies. They didn't speak. This had been agreed. If something *was* in the castle, or two somethings *were* in the castle, then it would be best to be silent.

They listened. Rooks cawed among the tall trees on the mainland where Anaglypta dozed over a sketch pad. The water made kissing noises against the bank.

Freddie looked at Lindsay. Her intent blue gaze examined every bit of grass, every shadow beneath the trees and tangled bushes, every crumbling stone of the ruin. Freddie did the same. A duck swam close to them, clambered over the grass, had a look at Freddie's toe and disappeared into the castle.

"Well," said Freddie, partly relieved and

partly disappointed, "there's nothing —"

His eyes widened and he shut his mouth firmly to keep from talking, for out of the castle came a single terrified *squawk!*

Lindsay's hand gripped Freddie's wrist. For a moment neither of them moved. Then Lindsay went very quietly, very cautiously, very *scaredly*, towards the tumbledown wall.

She peered over. Her hand thrust back at Freddie and the message in the upturned palm and rigid fingers was *stay still!*

But he didn't.

He couldn't! He simply couldn't! He had to see! It was his snake! Or elephant. He moved close to Lindsay and held her hand – partly to let her know he was there, partly because he was pretty shaky.

Then...

By gum, he had reason to shake!

As he inched his eyes over the wall, he saw more walls, a jumble of fallen stones, things growing ... and in the grass ... sliding rapidly through the grass ... the thickest, darkest, roundest, strongest, most horrifying slithering thing he'd ever seen in his whole life!

Lindsay's fingers crushed his so hard he almost yelped, then she turned, her face pale and her eyes shocked beneath her dripping hair, and shivering and shuddering she led Freddie – who was also shivering and shuddering — across the warm grass, silently, oh, so silently down on their knees in the mud until the water would support them, then swimming gently, then less gently, then desperately, thrashing and foaming, and through the reeds and past the bushes and grabbed their clothes, grabbed Anaglypta and dragged her, staggering with fat and sleep, around the lake, over the lawn, up the stone stairs between the gardens, in the great Main Door, past the suits of armour and up into Lindsay's bedroom.

They flung themselves on to the bed leaving Anaglypta to collapse into a chair. They lay gasping, and crying "Oh!" with each breath.

"Have you ever seen anything so *disgusting?*" yelled Lindsay at the canopy over her head. Then she sat up and leaned against the bedpost. "My legs are trembling," she said.

Freddie's legs were trembling too. He guessed he'd just broken the world record for swimming *and* running! He didn't know what to say to Lindsay. He certainly wasn't going to say, I told you so.

"Freddie Faucet," said Lindsay breathlessly, "you can punch me for calling you a liar."

"Where could it have come from?" he wanted to know.

Lindsay shook her head making her wet hair jiggle. "That's not the only problem," she said. "*What was the other thing you saw?* If you saw the snake, then you saw the elephant. But there simply *wasn't* an elephant! We would have seen anything that size."

"I suppose it could have been behind a wall. I mean, we didn't really look."

"*I* jolly well looked! I jolly well looked jolly hard! If something that big *had* been there I would have seen bushes or trees moving *at least!* It wasn't there! So *where is it?*"

"Where's what!" gasped Anaglypta. "You beasts! Where's what? You woke — You dragged me away from my sketching. I suppose it's one of your stupid beastly games! I'm a guest, you know, and must be treated with proper respect! I've a good mind to tell Uncle Alec and have you two in detention for a week!"

"That will suit us very well!" snapped Lindsay, turning on Anaglypta. "We'll be in detention here, and you'll be left on your own, and serve you right! You ungrateful pig! We've just saved your fat life and all you do is moan! You spend half your life asleep and half stuffing your face! Go and tell Alec, you blot! Go and tell, and I'll never speak to you again! You can spend the rest of the holidays on your own!"

Freddie was almost as frightened of Lindsay as Anaglypta was. He had never seen her so enraged. Perhaps it was because she was scared.

Anaglypta didn't understand half what Lindsay said because, of course, she hadn't seen the snake. All she knew was she'd been made to run half a mile, which was a hundred times further than she'd ever run before. She began to cry.

Lindsay turned sharply from her.

"I'll get dressed," said Freddie, and gathered up his clothes.

He went to his own room. His feet were grubby from running through the grass. He was sweaty and pond weed clung to his skin, so he took a shower. He wondered where his dressing room was. Lindsay said he had a sitting room too. Perhaps there were more secret doors.

Drying himself roughly, he looked round the bathroom. No door there. He wandered into his bedroom. There were no more mirrors that could hide doors, but there were an awful lot of wooden panels on the walls! In fact, wooden panels covered the walls almost to the ceiling! To think he hadn't noticed that before! Everything had been so exciting, he just couldn't take it all in!

Then on the wall opposite the mirror-door, he saw a round wooden handle. It was nearly invisible against the panels. He pulled on his clothes and turned the handle.

He found his sitting room. It too faced the lawn and the lake, and had the same balcony as his bedroom. It was a little smaller though, and very comfortable with settees and soft chairs and a very cosy fireplace. He imagined relaxing at the fire, logs burning, snow on the balcony, a mug of cocoa and a pile of comics – and his blood thrilled as he realized that he would, he really, really, *would* be here in the winter!

He said, "Yippee!" and dashed through to watch the three Freddies brushing their dark red hair. "This is our home!" he told them, and they smiled delightedly.

And then...

Well.

10

It was just a little noise. It was the tiniest, slightest little noise in the world.

Freddie turned away from the mirrors and stared at the secret door to his sitting room. The door was open a crack, just as he'd left it.

He heard the noise again.

A rustling.

A scrabbling.

A slidy noise of something dry being pushed or pulled, and the most incredibly meagre clink like tiny sharp things clicking on tiles, as if something with claws...

Very slowly, Freddie crossed the bedroom.

Very, very slowly he pushed the door, until it was open more than a crack. He put his eyes to the opening. He could see the window. He could *hear* the noise. It seemed to be coming from the fireplace. Was it only soot dropping on to the hearth? To see properly he'd have to open the door enough to get his head through. He pushed slowly.

Slowly.

He pressed his face into the space, with his ears squashed. Another tiny push...

Oh, no! The door creaked! It rotten-well *creaked!*

Then came a scuttling, scraping, rustling, rasping, clatter of noise...!

Freddie pushed the door wide and swung in.

Something moved in the fireplace. Something dark. Something scrabbling desperately, and soot flowed on to the hearth and carpet, billowing in a silent explosion across the room. Freddie had no choice but to step back and shut the door.

Slam! He stood with his heart thundering. He was panting. What had he seen?

Was it another snake?

A snake in the house?

A dark wriggling horror, living in *his house!*

Freddie shuddered. It couldn't be! It simply couldn't!

He ran to get Lindsay. He threw himself into her room, and she turned, a silver hairbrush held against her head.

"Lindsay!"

Anaglypta was still in the chair vibrating with snores.

"What is it?" said Lindsay, her eyes wide.

"I . . ."

Freddie had intended to say he'd seen something else — a third thing. First an elephant, then a snake, then . . . ? It was going to sound awfully far-fetched.

He blinked, undecided. He didn't want Lindsay's terrible stare on him again. She put the hairbrush on her dressing-table and stood close to him, looking down slightly.

"Have you seen it again?"

"No."

"Then what's wrong?"

"I saw something else. My sitting room's full of soot."

"*Soot!*"

"It's all over the place."

"Is that all? It happens. A bird gets in the chimney, or the wind swirls down. Don't get excited. Just tell Alec and he'll see to it. Have you had a bath? We can go to the library if you like, until lunch —"

"There was a thing in the fireplace!"

"Yes, a bird."

"It was too big."

"Have you seen a bird close up?"

"Of course."

"Really close? D'you know what size a crow is?"

"That size," said Freddie, measuring the air with his hands.

"*That* size!" said Lindsay, pushing his hands three times as wide. "With wings out, they're that size."

"It wasn't a bird."

"Then what was it? An elephant!"

"If you don't believe me..."

"I do, Freckles! I'm only teasing! What was it?"

"I don't know. I didn't really see it."

"Then how d'you know it wasn't a bird!"

"It didn't flutter! I tell you it was that size!" And he held out his hands again.

"One of the cats?" said Lindsay.

Freddie shook his head. "I don't know."

"Where did it go? Where is it now?"

"It went up the chimney."

"A cat wouldn't go up the chimney. They keep out of dirt. Let's look."

She went past Freddie, and he followed reluctantly.

"Be careful," he said, as she reached for the door. She pushed it open and marched in. A pile of soot had spilled from the hearth on to the carpet. A fine black film darkened the rest of the carpet and the furniture.

"Stay out," said Lindsay. She crossed to the fireplace and peered in, then she shrugged and came back to the door.

"Nothing," she said, and with one hand on the doorframe she pulled off her shoes and stepped into Freddie's bedroom. Then she walked in her socks to his bathroom. "I'll wash the soles," she told Freddie. "Staff hate cleaning up sootfalls, and don't jolly well appreciate extra, trodden into other rooms. I'll meet you in the library." Then she shot out before Freddie could remind her that he hadn't a clue where the library was!

Lindsay!

11

Lindsay had disappeared so definitely that Freddie felt it simply wouldn't be right to go after her.

He sighed. Then he smiled. For a moment he'd been hurt because she'd dashed off, then he realized why she'd dashed off. He – Freddie Faucet – was not a guest to be treated politely. *He* was family! Terrific!

He spent a minute looking for his dressing room and found it behind the panelling on the same wall as his bathroom. Its single window opened on to the balcony. He walked along the balcony crunching on arms of ivy. He peered into his own bedroom then, rather cautiously, into his sitting room. Everything was the same. Soot in the hearth. Lindsay's clean footprints on the darkened carpet.

The end of the balcony stopped him, but another started so close he could easily have clambered on to it and rattled Lindsay's window. He turned and scrunched along to the other end. A wider gap separated him from the next balcony. Down through the gap he could see into windows which came out at an angle. He saw bookshelves. The problem of finding the library was solved. All he had to do was go down the main stairs and keep to the front of the house.

He went to Lindsay's room and wakened Anaglypta. "We're meeting in the library," he told her. "You'd better wash your face, it's all tear stains."

"Why are we going to the library? I don't want to go to the library!"

Freddie just said, "I'll wait outside." He really couldn't be bothered with cousin Anaglypta.

When she came out, her face was slightly cleaner, but scowling. "I'm not going to the library! Where's Lindsay? I want to go to the cellar!"

"Lindsay's already in the library, and the cellar's out of bounds." Freddie walked towards the stairs.

"I want to see the cellar!" cried Anaglypta. "Oh, do come on!"

Freddie led the way, and found Lindsay hidden in a large chair at the library window. She wasn't reading but staring at the island in the lake.

The library walls were thick with books. High up was a narrow gallery running round the room to let you reach books near the ceiling. Fastened to the underside of the gallery was a brass rail. Freddie wondered if it was for curtains, then he noticed the ladders. At each wall was a beautiful ladder made of brass and wood. The ladders were on wheels and fastened at the top to the brass rail. Freddie pushed one and it slid along with a marvellous gliding motion.

"Where's Anaglypta?" asked Lindsay, uncurling from the chair.

"She was here a minute ago," said Freddie from halfway up a ladder.

"She's not on the gallery," said Lindsay.

"She kept on about the cellar..."

"Come on!"

Lindsay ran.

Freddie jumped to the polished floor. "What's the matter?" he shouted after her.

"It's out of bounds, that's what's the matter! She'll get us detention for a week!"

She raced down the stone stairs to the kitchen, jumping the last six steps. Freddie did the same and stung his feet. They clattered past Anaglypta's loo, dashed along a narrow cool passage, round a bend to the right, up three steps, along a tiled hallway, left, right, up, down, down again and bumped to a halt against a modern steel door.

Everywhere were whitewashed walls and ceilings.

Lindsay took a key from a box in the wall and with two hands screwed it round slowly in the lock. There was a loud click-thump and the steel door swung inwards.

"Oh," said Freddie.

He had expected darkness and cobwebs. He was rather disappointed at seeing more whitewashed walls, and electric lights were flickering on through a confusion of pillars, and walls, with openings rather than doors. It was very modern.

"This bit's been rebuilt over the years," said Lindsay.

"Who put on the lights?"

"They come on automatically when the door's opened."

"You had to unlock the door," Freddie pointed out. "If Anaglypta had come in, it would have been open."

Lindsay was leading him among the walls and pillars. They passed a huge glittering engine. "A generator for electricity," said Lindsay. "Anaglypta would come in the only way she knows. This is quicker. Maybe we can head her off."

There were walls only three feet high to clamber over.

"But why are we hurrying?" Freddie was panting. "We're out of bounds now anyway, so —"

"Freddie Faucet!" yelled Lindsay as she pulled herself up a metal ladder. "You just do as I say or you'll find a punch on the end of your freckly nose! I know this house..." She scuttled along a low passageway, then began to disappear downwards. She was on another ladder. "And until you know it like I do, you jolly well follow my lead!"

Freddie smiled as he half slid down the ladder. Lindsay's rows, he realized, always made him feel part of the family. He bounded along.

"Underneath this cellar," gasped Lindsay, "are more cellars. Anaglypta knows the way in. She was at me all last summer to show her. It's dangerous down there, Freddie — *more dangerous than the island!*" She stopped, hands on her denim knees, hauling in air. Freddie collapsed on to the cold stone floor. "Down there," Lindsay gasped, "she could get lost. It's real cellars, Freddie. All stone archways and dark tunnels. There are cobwebs as big as curtains and no light except for a string of temporary ones Alec put in last year — and they only go fifty metres. Ten years ago one of our workmen went down alone. *He never came out!* Now, *move!*"

And with panic chilling his blood, Freddie launched himself after his cousin. If a grownup could get lost for ever — for absolutely ever! — then Anaglypta could get lost twice as long!

They came to an open space.

It had the same white walls, but in one wall, looking very business-like and determined, was a little door also made of steel, about two feet above the floor. There would be just enough room for a man to squeeze through. The door had one, two, three, four, yes four! large bolts, but... The bolts had been pulled back and *the door was open!*

Freddie saw something on the edge of the wall which was really the bottom of the doorway. He pointed to it silently. "A corner of biscuit," said Lindsay. "She must have raided the biscuit barrel in my bedroom."

Beyond the door was darkness.

Lindsay stared in, leaning on the sill. She hesitated.

"Shouldn't we get help?" said Freddie anxiously.

"I'm not doing detention for her!" snapped Lindsay and clambered over. "Steps going down," she warned.

They descended into a glow of light.

It was dusty.

The roof slanted at the same angle as the steps.

It was dirty.

At the bottom a single row of bulbs with wire looped between them spread yellow circles on the floor. For a second Freddie remembered his bus journey and the up-and-down telephone lines.

There was a strange smell of ancientness.

A terrible silence hung among the shadows.

"Where can she be?" whispered Freddie.

They stared all around.

"Anaglypta," said Lindsay, not too loudly.

"Anaglypta," whispered the shadows.

"Anaglypta-ta-ta-ta..."

And the next thing made Freddie's dark red hair stand on end.

It made Lindsay's eyes as big as blue saucers!

It made Freddie grab Lindsay and Lindsay grab Freddie!

It —

12

Scream!

Scream upon scream!

Right beside them, *scream, scream, screammmmmmmm!*

They fled! They fled towards the stair.

Their legs couldn't go fast enough! Their hearts couldn't beat faster! They hit the bottom step.

"Anaglypta!" shrieked Lindsay. "It's Anaglypta! We've got to go back!" And the darkness howled, "Back, back, back, ack, kack..." Lindsay's fingers dug deep into Freddie's arm, and they turned and stared in terror. Beneath the row of bulbs came...

"Anaglypta!" whispered Lindsay.

Anaglypta had no more breath to cry out. She was running faster than Freddie would have believed possible.

"Get up to the door!" commanded Lindsay. "I'll help her!" Freddie did as she said. He went into the bright, white-walled place and held the door open. Anaglypta's ginger frizz appeared.

Her face was pale with terror and tears flowed leaving muddy streaks. She was gasping hoarsely and her fat-filled eyes were wide.

The doorway was too narrow!

"She got *in!*" yelled Lindsay. "Pull!"

Freddie caught Analgypta's head – which was the only part he could hold – and pulled. She plopped out, fell over the sill and rolled like a dusty barrel across the floor. Lindsay followed, Freddie slammed the door and pushed in all four bolts. They sat gasping.

Anaglypta was flat on her back again, moaning and puffing like an old steam train. Despite his fear, Freddie couldn't help thinking how horrible she looked.

"Let's get out of here," said Lindsay. She clicked a switch beside the door. "That's the lights off down there. Now go! *Go!*"

They pulled Anaglypta by the armpits. They dragged her hooting with pain over low brick walls. They pushed her through the low passageway and she ran staggering, encouraged by pinching and thumps from Lindsay.

Then they were out of the cellars and Lindsay prodded her dust-covered cousin to the nearest bathroom and shoved her in.

"If you're not clean," she hissed, her teeth gritted with fury, "by the time I come back with a dress, I will personally scrub every inch of your blubber with a soapy brick! *Oh!*" And she marched off, her eyes, thought Freddie, leaving scorch marks on the walls. He ran after her.

"When we get back to civilisation," said Lindsay, meaning the parts of the house with people, "keep out of sight. If I'm as dusty as you, they'll guess we've been in the cellar, then we'll be up to our necks in real trouble!"

"I wonder why she was screaming," said Freddie.

"We'll find out later. D'you know it isn't even lunch time yet? We'll need to get cleaned up. Take your time. I'll see to Anaglypta — the great pudding!"

She was quiet until they got to their corridor.

"Freckles," she said, "tell me again what you saw in the fireplace."

Freddie was surprised. He'd thought she didn't believe him.

"Just something dark about the size of a cat. I think it was rounder."

"Rounder?"

"Fatter."

"You're sure about the size?" Lindsay stared at the carpet. She held her hands out at full stretch. "Are you sure it wasn't that size?" she asked, her blue eyes focusing solemnly on Freddie's.

"Goodness, no! It couldn't have got into the fireplace! Why are you asking?"

Lindsay sat on the edge of their giant chair. She looked at him, then glanced away. There were cobwebs in her hair.

"After I told you to go up the stair I turned to grab Anaglypta. I saw something. Crouching in the shadows. Something alive.

It was moving — sort of snuffling about. I couldn't make out what it was, but … it was awfully big… Freddie, *it was awfully big!*"

13

The glass door of the kitchen lay wide to the summer day. Glittering cutlery lined a table, and plates were full of the colours of salads and meats. Tall and short glasses sparkled with good things to drink. And to finish preparations chairs were clattered out by an energetic Lindsay, an enthusiastic Freddie and a complaining Anaglypta.

"It's called a picnic, Anaglypta," said Lindsay. "You're supposed to enjoy it."

The sun stood hot in the middle of the courtyard and transparent shadows leaned out from the buildings. Alec and Alexandra appeared and Freddie was jolly glad they didn't ask questions. They tended to talk to each other or listen politely to anything the children said to them, otherwise Lindsay's chatter and Freddie's comments went unheard. Anaglypta's mouth was too busy to speak.

Afterwards they cleared up, then dragged Anaglypta a little way down the earthen road, where they sat on the grassy bank and turned their faces to the sun.

"Council of War," said Lindsay suddenly. "We must decide what to do."

"I'm going to sleep," scowled Anaglypta.

"You're going to talk!" snapped Lindsay.

"Sit up! Now tell us what you saw in the cellar!"

Anaglypta's little pink lip stuck out and her fat eyes closed up as if she were considering crying.

"If you blub..."

"I won't! But..."

"Why didn't you answer when I called?"

"I was hiding. You wouldn't let me go to the cellar. You're so selfish! So I just went myself. Why should I have to wait for you? I don't need you two following me around!"

"You weren't scared?" asked Freddie. He was amazed, really, that Anaglypta *had* gone into the cellar by herself.

"Course not!"

"Of course she wasn't," cried Lindsay, "because she was only in seconds before we were! She heard us coming and kept out of sight. I'll bet you waited until we were at the door, *then* you hid!"

Anaglypta scowled at the grass. "I was there ages!" she whined. "And I wasn't a bit scared! The dark doesn't scare me!"

Lindsay shook her head in disbelief. "If you weren't scared," she said cuttingly, "it's because you're too stupid to know the danger. D'you know what's beyond the lights? Archways. Archways, archways and archways! And they all look the same. In some places there are passages and rooms. There are places with the roof so low that you have to lie flat to get under! If you weren't scared it's because you're an idiot! Oh, put your lip away! Don't you ever think of anything but eat, sleep and blub? Tell us why you screamed. Now!"

Anaglypta was trying to control her breathing. "I saw a ghost."

"A ghost!" gasped Freddie.

"It came down out of the dark and looked at me. You'd have screamed!"

Lindsay's terrible gaze sharpened on to Anaglypta.

"Are you fibbing?" she asked coldly.

"You would have screamed! You ran away! You selfish beasts ran off and left me!"

Lindsay's stare silenced Anaglypta.

"Describe the ghost," commanded Lindsay.

"I just have!"

"Again!"

"It . . . it was whitish. It came out of the sky —"

"Sky!"

"The roof! It crawled along the floor and watched me!"

"What size was it?"

Anaglypta's fat arms waved. "Big. Big."

"How big? As big as you?"

"Bigger! Well. . ."

"You mean smaller. How much smaller?"

"I don't know." Angaglypta scowled.

"If you don't know you must be really stupid!"

"I'm not!"

"Then tell me what size it was!"

"It was..." Anaglypta's eyes slid around
reluctantly. It was obvious to Freddie that the
ghost wasn't big at all.

"About that size," she said at last, nodding
her ginger frizz at a stone.

"Bigger than you," murmured Lindsay.
"You imagine, do you, you're smaller than
a football? The same shape, Anaglypta, but
hardly the same size. Is that all?"

Anaglypta held her lip with her teeth and
shrugged her beefy shoulders.

"Next," said Lindsay, "is the snake."

"Snake!"

"Not here! On the island. That's why we
dragged you away this morning. There's a
snake on the island as long as a bus."

Anaglypta laughed. She laughed a fat-
quivering laugh. A silly hee-hee-hee that
swallowed her eyes and wobbled her body.

Lindsay stared, and Freddie stared. Neither
of them had seen Anaglypta laugh. She really
was foul.

"She doesn't believe you," said Freddie.

"We both saw it!" snapped Lindsay. "Oh,
stop cackling! You're like a half-witted chick-
en!"

Anaglypta turned on a scowl and waddled

away. She sprawled under a tree and dozed off.

"Good," said Lindsay. "Now we can plan what we're going to do."

"We really should tell someone," said Freddie.

"Tell someone! They would laugh like she did! And anyway, it's our mystery. We'll solve it ourselves. And don't you tell anyone Freddie Faucet or —"

"All right!" said Freddie. "But what can we do? You saw the size of that snake."

"I've been thinking about that," said Lindsay. She lay back on the grass, her eyes closed against the sun, her denim knees in the air. "What if it wasn't a snake? Did you see its head?"

"What else could it be? No, but..."

"Listen, Freckles, as far as I know there's no such thing as a grey-brown snake that long."

"It was all scaly."

"I *know*! But it doesn't make sense! Where could it have come from? If it had escaped from a zoo, someone would be searching. Why haven't we seen it anywhere else? Oh, Freddie, it just didn't *feel* like a snake!"

Freddie knew what she meant. He hadn't thought of it, but now Lindsay pointed it out, there *was* something wrong. It didn't feel right. It didn't feel right at all!

14

"So what have we got?" said Lindsay. She stuck out her thumb. "We've got an elephant."

She stuck out a finger. "A giant snake."

She stuck out another finger. "A thing in the fireplace."

She stuck out a third finger. "A thing in the cellar, bigger than the thing in the fireplace."

She stuck out her pinkie. "A ghost. That's five things."

"And the sounds in the chimneys," added Freddie.

"That was the wind," she whispered.

She had been looking at Freddie while she talked. Then she lowered her hand and glanced away.

Freddie, once again, felt that Lindsay knew something she wasn't telling – something she wouldn't admit to him – something she wouldn't even admit to herself.

She jumped up and wandered off as if she didn't like the silence – as if she knew he was going to ask a question she didn't want to answer.

"It's all so silly!" she said loudly.

"You told me," said Freddie, "you couldn't stand a liar in the house. Is not telling the same as lying?" He relaxed, hands behind his head, sun on his eyelids, his tummy full of picnic. He heard Lindsay's feet approaching through the grass. He felt her shadow as she sat down.

"It's mice," she said quietly. "I hate them. They give me the shudders. You haven't been here long enough to know, but our house is called Mouse Hall. Not that there are more mice here than anywhere else, but... Oh..."

Freddie opened an eye cautiously against the sunlight. Lindsay was on her side twisting grass round her fingers.

"Every hundred years there's supposed to be a *change*. For some reason that no one knows, bigger mice appear. No one's ever seen one, of course, because no one's old enough to remember and, really, very few people believe it, but... There are books in the library, some a century old, some ancient, going away back to the days of the abbey before Mouse Hall was built – the castle is really part of the abbey buildings – it's nearly a thousand years old..."

"Golly!" said Freddie quietly.

"We've talked about it often with Mr James – he's our biology teacher – and he said it wasn't impossible for a freak genetic strain to appear now and then, but it would die away naturally for a whole lot of reasons – not enough food, was one."

Lindsay sighed. "The lake was made after

the last time. People were afraid of the ruin. Animals and birds were disappearing from the woods. Every one of the peacocks vanished. It was Alec who brought our peacocks from India. Even sheep and cattle were left on the hillsides as piles of bones. One book says that children never came home after being out alone. Freddie, that was a hundred years ago."

She pulled anxiously at his arm. Her eyes were wide with horror. "They've come back!" she whispered.

Freddie stared at her. His hair seemed to be trying to stand on end and chills clung to his back like wet jelly. "Do you think," he said, "the elephant I saw..."

Lindsay nodded. "It was an enormous mouse!"

"An Enormouse!" gasped Freddie. "But what about the snake! The scaly dark snake!"

"Of course! I told you it didn't feel right! *That's* what it was! The tail! The tail of the Enormouse!"

"But it was scaly!"

"Yes! A mouse's tail *is* scaly! Don't you see, Freckles! Every one of these things — in the fireplace! In the cellars! Every one was a mouse! And counting the elephant, that makes three! At least three! One fully grown, a medium one in the cellar and a cat-sized one in the fireplace. And who knows how many more! Oh, golly!" Lindsay jumped up. "We've got to do something!"

"But what? And what about Anaglypta's ghost? How could that have been a mouse?"

"I don't know. Maybe she dreamed it. Freddie we've got to tackle this ourselves! Can you imagine what grown-ups would say!"

"But —"

"Listen. It's up to us. We've got to get proof — absolute proof — that the Enormouse is back! Anything less will just get us laughed at!"

"But if we tell the truth —"

"If we tell them what we've seen they won't believe it! Don't you know anything about grown-ups? They only believe what they want to believe! Freddie," announced Lindsay solemnly, "we must go back to the island."

Freddie blinked. Lindsay's mouth was suddenly very firm and all the fear had gone from her eyes. She stared hard at Freddie and he saw that Lindsay Dundas would never again shudder at the sight of a mouse.

15

"If you squeal," said Lindsay menacingly, "I'll throw you overboard and stick you headfirst in the mud."

Anaglypta was jammed in the back of the skiff and Freddie was at the bow. The little boat had been hanging on the wall of the boathouse and it had taken the three of them to lift it down and lower it into the water.

Lindsay was pulling the oars with slow, silent-dipping, water-gripping strokes that sped them towards the island – but on the side away from Mouse Hall, so they wouldn't be seen.

"No more talking," commanded Lindsay.

Freddie pointed binoculars at the island. It was only a couple of cricket-pitch lengths away, but his detailed view of tree bark and writhing ivy on ancient stone gave him confidence that he could see everything that was to be seen.

Lindsay back-watered the oars and the skiff slowed and swung against the grassy bank. Freddie climbed out silently and held the wooden rim. He helped Anaglypta on to the grass, reminding her, with a finger on his lips, to be quiet. Lindsay rested the oars. Freddie tied the rope – the painter, as Lindsay called it – to the stem of a shrub.

They stood still, looking, listening. Rooks cawed among trees on the mainland. On the island, nothing moved. It was as if the creatures of lake and shore had learned the danger and left the island to the trees and tumbling stones.

Lindsay walked carefully to the place where she could see over the ruined wall. A thousand years old, thought Freddie excitedly. He couldn't take that in! He stood close to Lindsay and peered at the inside of the castle.

Last time he had stood here he had seen little but the awful snake. Now he had time to notice that there wasn't much of the castle left at all, and that even when built, it had been pretty small. Only the outer walls were still high. The inside walls were just rows of stones on the ground and so tumbledown it was impossible to say exactly where the walls had been. Bushes, grass and wild flowers, and even tall trees grew up through the ruins.

Lindsay pointed at a tree. It looked as if someone had hacked off the bark with an axe. The inside lay white and bare and, round about, the grass, the flowers, even the bushes, were trampled and crushed as if something very heavy had walked up and down many, many times.

Freddie could see the plants were flattened all the way into the castle tower, but what was inside the tower he scarcely dared think!

Then, very quietly, Lindsay led the way around the wall, over the trampled grass, past the tree with its bare white wood and cautiously, ever so cautiously, closer and closer to the shadowy place inside the tower!

Oh, golly!

Oh, boy!

Oh, *good grief!*

16

"Oh!" gasped Anaglypta, and Freddie and Lindsay were so utterly amazed that they forgot to hush her, for there in front of them inside the tower, hidden by the tower walls and surrounded by great heaps of trampled earth was the biggest, blackest, deepest-looking hole in the ground any of them had ever seen!

Lindsay's blue eyes opened very wide indeed, Freddie's mouth gaped and Anaglypta — after saying, "Oh!" — stepped back hastily, slipped a little,
leaned on Freddie, who
leaned on Lindsay, who
being nearest the edge of the hole, turned and grabbed Freddie, who
turned and grabbed Anaglypta, who
leaned even more on Freddie and
Freddie simply *had* to lean on Lindsay —
and Lindsay's eyes grew even wider. She bit her lip as she tried not to cry out! Then!
Oh, no!
Not Lindsay!
LINDSAY VANISHED INTO THE HOLE!!!

SHUT THE BOOK!

GO TO BED!

IT'S *TOO*

TERRIBLE!!!

Children are advised to stick
the pages of Part Two together
with jam, to prevent parents
from reading further. It
really is too exciting for
older people.

Hugh Scott

Part Two

1

Freddie couldn't help it!

He cried out! It was against their own rules, but no one, absolutely no one in the world, could have stood and watched someone he cared about fall into that hole and stayed silent. The only person who just might have done it was Lindsay Dundas, for she hadn't cried out even when *she* fell into the hole!

Anaglypta, of course, started to blub. And when Anaglypta blubbed, Freddie smiled. His smile widened into a huge grin! And his huge grin turned into a gigantic sigh of relief!

For when Anaglypta blubbed, up out of the darkness came a voice hissing, "Freddie Faucet, if you don't silence that yowling barrel of lard I'll feed you both to the Enormouse limb by limb! Get me out of here!"

Lindsay!

"Lindsay!" whispered Freddie. "I can't see you! Where are you?"

"Down here, of course! I can see you well enough. It's too deep to climb out. I slithered in! Get something I can hold on to! And for goodness' sake, shut up!"

Freddie hauled off his sweatshirt, threw himself flat on the trampled earth and let the sleeves dangle into the hole at arm's length.

"Can you reach that?" he hissed.

He felt a tug.

He gripped the sweatshirt tightly and signalled at Anaglypta to hold his other arm. The shirt was slipping from his fingers, then Lindsay's warm hand clamped his wrist in the darkness. Then she was pulling herself up his arm, clutching his neck and pushing his face in the dirt.

Freddie rolled over and smiled up at her. His heart was thumping now the danger was over. Lindsay's look wiped away his smile. Without a sound she pointed her command to Move! And she marched off past the stripped tree, round the castle wall, across the grassy bank and into the rocking skiff.

It wasn't until the skiff was tethered in the boathouse that she spoke. Freddie had been too scared to speak and Anaglypta too busy snuffling.

"You idiots!" she snarled, and her voice echoed under the boathouse roof. "You blundering, balloon-footed ninnies! You've ruined the mission! You spoiled everything! What a noise! That thing down there could have heard us and come charging out! What chance d'you think we'd have had? D'you think we'd have made it to the skiff? You saw the teeth marks on the tree! This isn't some game we're playing! It's an investigation! And it's got to be done properly! Another mistake could cost us our lives!"

She swung away, strode from the boat-house and along the lakeside path.

Freddie knew she was right. They had been clumsy and another mistake could be disastrous. He led the sniffling Anaglypta after Lindsay, beneath the trailing arms of willows.

Rooks still cawed in the tall trees. The water rippled in gentle rings around the island. A fish plopped close to shore. Lindsay was striding across the lawn. Freddie ran and caught up with her.

"What do you want to do before dinner?" he asked.

Lindsay slowed to a normal walk and glanced at him. Her temper never lasted.

"We'll go for a swim," she said. She looked at Freddie from his hair to his toes, stared at Anaglypta with a silent groan, then grinned as she peered at herself. "We all need a shower, but we can do that at the pool. Anaglypta!" she yelled. "We'll meet you at the swimming pool! Remember your towel!" And she sped away leaving Freddie to catch up — and not bothering at all about the grumbling Anaglypta.

When Freddie reached the top of the main staircase, Lindsay was sitting in their double chair trying not to pant. She casually waved her towel at him. She had been in her room, found the towel and come out again! Lindsay could run!

Freddie got his towel.

"If we wait for Anaglypta," he said, "we'll never get a swim. We don't have to be *too* hosty, do we, and hang around?"

"She knows the way," said Lindsay, and led Freddie along the endless corridor away from the stairs. She pushed through two tall doors into another corridor far too wide and rich in furniture and curtains to *be* a corridor, then through more doors where dozens of Lindsays and Freddies leapt excitedly waving dozens of towels, for the walls were crammed with mirrors; then down a flight of stairs with a fireplace on the landing and at last plunged into a place as hot and sticky as a jungle.

It was very like a jungle. For a moment Freddie thought he was outside. Trees towered seeking a domed blue sky. Plants with gigantic leaves sweated in the still air. But the ground was made of tiles zigzagging between trunks and stems and the domed roof was clear glass looking down into a pool large enough for a tiled island, planted with palm trees, to stick up from the flat water...

"Wow!" said Freddie.

"Not bad," said Lindsay. "To be honest, we didn't pay for it. Three universities coughed up for the plants and maintenance. They send students down and you might find an odd professor pottering in the bushes. Choose a changing room," she told him, and vanished into the greenery.

Freddie rushed in a slightly different direction and found a changing room. It was bigger than the ones in a public pool. It had a sagging armchair, a rug, green tiles to the ceiling, a little door – Freddie peered in – golly! a shower and toilet!

What a place!

What a fantastic place!

He stripped off his earthy clothes, showered, pulled on his trunks without drying himself – which wasn't easy – and ran through the jungle towards the pool. Lindsay sprang from between the trees and with a tremendous echoey yell leapt high in the air and hit the water with a fountainous splash! Freddie followed so closely that his splash was going up while Lindsay's was coming down!

"Race you round the island!" cried Lindsay, and Freddie followed her. He kept up easily, but because Lindsay swam in a curve he couldn't overtake, so she touched the poolside triumphantly.

But Freddie knew he could beat her.

He pulled himself on to the tiles, turned on his toes and dived in. He rose close to the island and was astonished to see a table and chairs on it among the shrubbery. Then he ducked and swam deep and was astonished again to find he could swim under the island because a marvellous sculptured shape supported it. Then what should he see, but fish.

Freddie stared. Never had he heard of a swimming pool with fish! The fish were at the wall of the pool. He swam forwards slowly underwater. Then he realized – they weren't in the pool at all! They were in a long glass tank built under the edge. He gazed in fascination at their masses of moving colour, then came up gasping!

He gasped some more. Anaglypta was walking through the trees. Her ginger frizz clung to her scalp with water. She had done the same as Freddie – showered and pulled on her costume without drying herself. Freddie couldn't think how she managed. He'd had a struggle to get his trunks over his legs, but Anaglypta!

Freddie sank beneath the surface and a pink and green fish blew bubbles at him. He felt sorry for Anaglypta, but he couldn't help staring. He made a face at the fish, pushed off from the glassy wall, slid twisting through the island sculpture, then climbed underwater steps up to the table and chairs. He sprawled on a chair. Lindsay was swimming towards him with a floating tray. Freddie was beginning to think he'd spend the rest of his life staring. A floating cork tray! And on it, three giant cups half full of something milky-brown and steaming!

"Coffee!" said Lindsay.

"Gosh!" said Freddie. He knelt down and lifted the cups on to the table.

"Coffee, Anaglypta!" called Lindsay. "You'll have to swim for it!"

Anaglypta descended tiled steps until the water was at her chin, then to Freddie's amazement, pushed off, and swam with an elegant breast stroke, her little pink mouth spouting water. She climbed on to the island.

"Jolly well done!" said Lindsay, and pulled herself up by the stem of a giant rubberplant. They chattered over their coffee, Anaglypta joining in confidently, after her swim; and the coffee, Freddie discovered, came from a coffee machine in the swimming pool's kitchen!

He nearly fell off his seat!

A kitchen in a swimming pool!

Wow!

In fact, wow! wow! wow!

Then they swam.

Anaglypta swam.

Lindsay swam.

Freddie swam. Only Freddie could dive. Lindsay would jump in. Anaglypta stayed in the water until dinner time.

Then at dinner...

Ah, dinner...

2

Freddie found more new clothes laid out on his four-poster. The shirt was plain but for a tiny mouse's head stitched on to the collar; a plain tie; new trousers and shoes. None of it, considered Freddie, grand enough for the Great Hall, but much too formal for the kitchen.

Where were they eating tonight?

He met Lindsay in the corridor. Her hair hadn't grown mysteriously but dashes of delicate green sparkled here and there on soft curls. Her dress was simple and she wore a wrap round her shoulders.

"Dinner on the roof," said Lindsay.

Freddie gaped.

Lindsay knocked on Anaglypta's door. "Dinner on the roof!" she called.

Anaglypta appeared, spotless for once after her swim. Her frizz had dried into tight orange curls. She too was wearing a wrap, but her dress was frilly.

Lindsay led the way.

First of all, they went *down*stairs. Then they went downstairs *again* to the kitchen. They went through a door Freddie hadn't used before – then up a not-very-wide staircase. It was a long way up. He was getting hot. Anaglypta was puffing.

"We'll use the lift," gasped Lindsay. And before Freddie could take in this new surprise, she climbed to the next landing and disappeared round a corner. She was prodding a button beside an old-fashioned lift gate. The lift clanked into sight as Anaglypta heaved herself on to the landing. "Pile in!"

Then they piled out on to the roof. "This is the main part of the house," said Lindsay. "Remember the iron ladder we didn't climb when we were playing on the rooftops? It leads up here."

Freddie was astonished. The sun shone on flowers. The flowers held out their petals and bees descended and rose like a traffic of fuzzy helicopters. Gardens on the roof! And a cage as big as a bedroom, crowded with canaries; yellow rows of them shuffling and chattering, bright as sunshine! And brick chimney stacks standing in front of long shadows. "Gosh!" whispered Freddie. And his mouth opened but he said nothing as he took in the view of endless miles of farmland and, close below, the great lawn rolling down to the lake with the thousand-year-old ruins.

Anaglypta poked her fingers in at the canaries then sat at the table.

This was a Semi-Formal, Lindsay explained. When it was too jolly hot to eat piles of grub or sit indoors in frilly shirts and jackets, they dined here in the roof garden. Gave the canaries company too. Made them sing better — then they brought a higher price. Alec's idea.

And did they enjoy it!

Right through to the end they enjoyed it!

Until...

Well, until...

Something very small...

3

No one noticed at first, but it appeared as if by magic on Lindsay's hand. A black speck. She rubbed it and it smeared. Soot.

Freddie saw her glance up. He looked first at the cage where the canaries were shuffling uneasily, then back at Lindsay. Her face hadn't moved at all, but something *changed*, for her glance froze, as hard and still as ice, then she switched her eyes to Freddie and nodded the tiniest nod towards Alec and Alexandra. It was a warning. As clear as words, it said, Don't attract their attention!

"The birds are making a devil of a noise," said Alec.

Freddie managed to turn the same way as Lindsay. He looked up. He stared at the chimneys on top of the nearest chimney stack. He knew his own face had that frozen stillness. But he couldn't help it.

Little bits of soot were tumbling down gently from a chimney pot, and there – peering towards the canary cages – was a sooty,

sharp-nosed,

round-eared,

bright-eyed,

Enormouse!

Freddie couldn't look away! The nose was sniffing nervously, then a paw appeared and combed the whiskers, scattering more soot into the still air. A chair scraped and the head vanished into the chimney.

"May we be excused?" said Lindsay firmly.

They crushed into the lift.

"But that was proof!" said Freddie. "If they'd seen it we wouldn't need to do anything else!"

"Exactly!" said Lindsay. "Don't you have any sense of adventure! Any sense of responsibility? This is our house, Freddie Faucet, and we have to look after it! We're only children, but we can still *do* things! If we leave it all to grown-ups how are we jolly well going to learn anything!"

Freddie hadn't thought of that.

"So, what now?"

"We prepare an Expedition!"

4

They strode into Lindsay's sitting room. It was the same size as Freddie's, but lived in, with books, posters, an old television set and a couple of lonely dolls. Anaglypta switched on the television.

"Put that off!" said Lindsay. "Now come here to the desk. I've started a list."

"A list?" said Freddie.

"Things we'll need for the expedition. Here's what I've got so far. Grub, lemonade . . ."

"But we'll only be a little while," said Freddie. "We're not going for days!"

"Have you ever heard of an expedition without supplies? Grub," repeated Lindsay, reading from the list, "lemonade, torches, string. What else?"

"What's the string for?"

"It's a guide line," explained Lindsay. "So we don't get lost."

"How can we get lost," sniffed Anaglypta, "on a little island?"

"We're going down the hole!" said Lindsay. "Why d'you think we need torches? Don't you know anything about what's going on? The Enormouse lives down the hole! It's a tunnel, and I'll bet it leads straight into this house!"

"Into the cellars!" gasped Freddie.

Lindsay nodded. "Where I saw the medium-sized one."

"And they must have passageways inside the walls that lead to some of the chimneys!"

"Right! Your brain's beginning to work, Freckles! Oh, yes. A rope to get into the hole."

"I won't go!" cried Anaglypta. "It's dark! It's got a ghost!"

"You said you weren't afraid of the dark! And you're going! We need everyone for this! And if you tell . . ."

Lindsay's blue glare turned on Anaglypta, and Anaglypta retreated into a giant leather chair and hid her face.

"We'd better take matches," said Freddie, "and something to burn. If we do meet the Enormouse . . . Well."

"Of course! We'd have to defend ourselves!" Lindsay thought for a moment. "Straw! We'll tie straw into bundles and we can light them and throw them! Good thinking!"

They sat silent while Lindsay wrote. Then she jumped up and rummaged in a drawer. She found a camera. "For evidence!" she exclaimed. "Yes, there's film in it and I've got a flash somewhere. Here! Wow! C'mon! We've lots to do!" And she dashed out into the corridor.

Well.

They were pretty busy; Lindsay urging Anaglypta to hurry up, Freddie working steadily. By bedtime they had half a dozen straw torches made, a rope with large knots in it for easy climbing and a supply of grub raided from the fridges and packed in plastic bags so each person could take enough for their own needs. Anaglypta, of course, would have packed grub all night if Lindsay hadn't restrained her.

They reckoned they'd thought of everything, for when they said goodnight in the corridor, and Lindsay – her face flushed with sun and sleepiness – asked, "Have we forgotten anything?" Anaglypta just grumbled about not being allowed to keep her supplies in her room and Freddie shook his head and went straight to bed.

They had thought of everything.

Almost.

5

They stood round the rim of the hole. The after-breakfast sun warmed the back of Freddie's neck. His tummy was full of bacon and egg, toast and marmalade. Tied to his belt was a bag of grub and two straw torches. An electric torch hung from his wrist on a loop of string (his own idea, in case it fell) and snug in his pocket, a box of matches.

Lindsay and Anaglypta carried the same; and each had extras. Anaglypta clutched the lemonade bottle, Lindsay the camera and Freddie the ball of string. Unknown to Lindsay, Freddie had an *extra* extra thrust into his belt. Over his shoulder hung the coiled climbing rope.

Lindsay signalled. Freddie tied the rope to a torn-off tree stump. She pointed into the hole. He lowered the rope quietly. They stood listening.

Lindsay handed the camera to Freddie and swung herself over the edge. Her fair hair descended into the darkness. Her torch flashed and Freddie dropped the camera down.

Anaglypta.

Freddie couldn't think how she would manage.

She put aside the lemonade, then lay flat, her feet over the edge. She clung to the rope where it crossed the ground and wriggled un-til her legs were dangling. Freddie waited ages while Anaglypta's feet found a knot to stand on. Then she slid her hands nearer the edge and her whole bulk went slowly into the pit. The fingers of her left hand stretched towards the lemonade. Freddie signalled impatiently at her to leave it.

It was over a minute before Anaglypta's torch told Freddie she was down. He was relieved and surprised. Anaglypta could do things when she really had to. He dropped the bottle to her, then the string. Freddie went down almost as fast as Lindsay. Two torches shone on the end of the rope. Freddie tied the string to it. Above, he could see only the rim of the hole and the hot sky. The torches swung away and their beams fingered the darkness.

6

They could see nothing. Freddie's torch made
an oval of light on the ground, and a little
bone glinted whitely and duck feathers wafted
as he passed. The floor sloped down. Lindsay
went first, then Anaglypta very close to her,
then Freddie unravelling the string.

The sky disappeared. The tunnel roof was
high above Freddie's head and dangled with
ancient roots. And the lake was up there. It
didn't feel good.

They went down and down. The air went
warmly into Freddie's mouth. It tasted of
mouse.

The ground was suddenly level. Freddie
reckoned they were halfway between the island and the shore, going towards the house.

Lindsay stopped and switched off Anaglypta's torch. Conserving light in this place was
sensible. They walked on, then Lindsay stopped again. There was a second tunnel.

They peered down it, stabbing the thick
darkness with two torch beams. It went deeper. Should they risk it, or go straight on?
Straight on meant towards the house. In the
dim glow beyond the beams, Lindsay's eyes
were wide and her face pale, but her mouth
was determined.

She stepped into the new opening.

Freddie tied a loop in the string so he would know this place again. He glanced back, but it was completely dark. He followed Lindsay and Anaglypta. The floor sloped steeply. Suddenly, under their feet was rock. The floor of the tunnel became very uneven, because, Freddie guessed, even the Enormouse couldn't dig through rock, so the shape of the rock decided the shape of the floor.

They climbed down by the light of their torches.

They clambered up. The camera glinted in Lindsay's hand. The lemonade bottle clinked on stone as Anaglypta struggled silently along. Once, the ball of string fell from Freddie's tense fingers and rolled away. He flashed the torch excitedly to make the others stop. Then he scrambled about desperately until he found the string, and they went on, hearts thumping.

It was getting stuffy. All three were gasping and the mousy smell was strong. Freddie wished they hadn't come. He hated that feeling of his back being naked to the darkness. But they went on.

Lindsay sat down. They had been descending for some time. She signalled Freddie to switch off his torch, then she switched off her own. It was terrible. They were smothered in blackness. Lindsay's torch came on.

Then they stood up, their feet sending

117

whispering echoes behind them.

Suddenly the sound changed. The echoes stopped. Lindsay's torch leapt from the floor and stabbed the darkness. The tunnel walls had vanished. Freddie searched with his light. It glanced on tips of rock and bulges from the roof.

Where were the walls?

He whirled, facing backwards. The light pressed its bright eye on a rocky cliff and showed him the mouth of a tunnel – the tunnel they'd just left. He was sweating. His light slid round, swelling on a pillar of rock, but before them and to either side, the stony landscape fell away into everlasting darkness. Freddie's fingers trembled as he tied a second loop in the string.

He knew they were in a cave, and the Enormouse's tunnel led to it by chance; or perhaps it was the other way round. Was this terrible place the original land of the Enormouse and had the creature burrowed *out* – out into their world of sunshine and rain and clean fresh air? He was longing to speak, to say his thoughts and have the warmth of someone else's words. Silence was lonely.

They crept across the endless floor. Pieces of rock waited, like dwarfs haunting the darkness and looming giants.

Freddie's torch shone on a slippery place. He knelt down and touched it, then flickered the light rapidly making Lindsay and Anaglypta turn. He walked his fingers on the stone, making the girls realize that something had passed here, often — very often — wearing down the surface.

They advanced nervously, Lindsay's light lancing ahead, investigating the blackness. She halted. She seemed to be listening. Her light darted anxiously, but only touched on rock, suddenly close, suddenly far away.

Freddie listened until his ears ached. It was hard to believe the noise was there. It was the sort of sound you only notice when it stops. They had come upon it slowly and accepted it as part of the silence. Lindsay was aware of it first.

A sighing in the darkness.

Like breathing.

Like someone sleeping and breathing.

But not quite. Not quite the simple sighing out and breathing in of a single sleeper. Maybe two or three...

Or four.

Or...

7

Freddie flicked off his torch. He fumbled with the string, tying another loop. He couldn't think what else to do. He was sweating all over, and darkness, outside the torchlight, pressed around him.

Lindsay's beam touched a rocky giant whose shadow slithered horribly. The light crept along a ridge.

Lindsay's hot palm found Freddie's wrist; her fingers closed on his skin and forced him down. He could feel Anaglypta clutching his elbow and knew she was afraid. They were all afraid.

Lindsay held her torch against the rocky floor leaving a tiny pool of light to move in, but none to spill through the emptiness...

They crawled forwards and peered over the ridge. The blackness touched Freddie's eyes. In the dreadful gloom rose breathing and sighing. They could hear it easily now they knew it was there.

Lindsay covered the torch with her hand, giving a blood-red outline to her fingers. Slowly, she brought it to the edge of the ridge. She turned it towards the sound. More rocks, dim, lower down and well worn. Something at the edge of the light shifted. Lindsay froze. With trembling care, she opened her fingers.

Freddie saw lumps. Pink lumps, naked and softly sighing. Enormouse babies!

Lindsay gasped. Anaglypta's nails dug into Freddie's arm. Freddie was sweating madly. He wondered if there was a parent about. He clicked on his torch and slid the light over the sleeping lumps, then on the rocks around them. A glimmer of bone here and there, and a scrap of fur. No parent. Thank goodness!

He nudged Lindsay and pushed the camera — which was hanging from her wrist — into her hand. She nodded and pointed it. The flash ripped open the darkness. Freddie saw nothing but green splodges. Then his eyes cleared.

The lumps wriggled. An eye stared into the torchlight and the sighing grew into snuffling and the snuffling into squeaking. Lindsay and Anaglypta made no attempt to move, but sat fascinated as the pink mound of babies heaved and mouthed tiny cries into the darkness.

Freddie knew the girls didn't realize the danger. He pulled at them but they crouched low, gaping and panting. He must speak. He put his mouth into Lindsay's hair. "The parents will come!" he whispered. "They'll hear the squealing!" To Anaglypta he simply hissed, "Run for your life!" And with three torches on, they scrambled up the rocks following the string.

To Freddie's astonishment they reached the previous loop in about a minute. They must have spent ages creeping a very short distance. That loop meant they were at the tunnel which had brought them into the cave. They were panting hard. Three fans of light flashed around searching. There it was! They hurried forward.

Then...

What was happening!

It wasn't possible!

It *just wasn't possible!*

8

From the tunnel blew a wind. Like a mighty, soft brush it swept them backwards down the rocks, clattering and crashing, scraping knees and bruising arms and backs. They landed in a tangle at the foot of the pillar.

Freddie's torch stayed lit. What a terrific idea tying the torches to their wrists had been.

The wind was less strong because they were further from the tunnel mouth but it hauled at their clothes, blew through their hair and dragged at the straw at their belts.

"Behind the pillar!" shouted Freddie. He hoisted Anaglypta to her feet. They dashed under cover just as the wind faded.

Freddie clicked off the torch. Anaglypta clung to his arm and he could feel her trembling with sobs, but even in that terrible moment his respect for her grew, for not once had she uttered a sound.

Lindsay held his hand and her grip tightened, for as the wind died, there rose such a roaring and grumbling, such a snuffling jumble of noise!

Like the noise deep down in the chimneys!
And a clatter like giant claws!
And a dreadful smell like a thousand mice!
Freddie wanted to scream! The floor vibrated as something devastatingly heavy

thundered past the far side of the pillar. A tremendous draught, like a bus going by, swirled around them, and Freddie understood the wind — it had been caused by the creature running madly down the tunnel, its great rounded body brushing the walls and roof, forcing the air ahead of it, as an underground train sends giant gasps into a station.

They didn't dare move.

The squeaking of the babies was louder. The grunting of the parent echoed dreadfully close, sounding almost solid in the blackness. They stood still for a very long time. The squeals became the sighing of sleep. The grunting softened to a hoarse wheeze. But it didn't go away.

Slowly, Freddie felt Anaglypta sinking. He released Lindsay's grip from his hand and she immediately clutched his shoulder. He guided Anaglypta to a sitting position. Silently, he pushed Lindsay down, then himself. Carefully they lay back, with the straw torches under their heads. Freddie breathed through his mouth. It was difficult in such stifling darkness to keep his eyes open. He didn't dare move. Minutes lingered. He felt Lindsay relax. Anaglypta breathed steadily. Freddie was quite sure he would stay awake...

It was so dark Freddie didn't know if he'd opened his eyes. He blinked, feeling his lashes with his palm. He wouldn't have believed darkness could be so complete!

He listened, wondering how long he'd been asleep. Lindsay and Anaglypta still clutched him through their dreams. Anaglypta was snoring gently.

The sighing of the Enormouse babies continued, but Freddie couldn't hear the parent. Was it still there? He had to know.

He eased free of Lindsay's grasp and Anaglypta's soft fingers, and stood up, gritting his teeth at the rustling of his clothes and straw torches. He stepped away from the pillar and it was only then he realized that he didn't have the ball of string.

He didn't have the ball of string!

His heart bumped with panic. Then he remembered. He'd had the string in his hand as they approached the tunnel. It must be nearby. Unless that unnatural wind had carried it miles into the darkness. It could be down a crevice or sunk in an underground pool! He told himself to stop guessing and look. He put his hand over the torch face as Lindsay had done, then — after listening for the parent Enormouse — switched on. He moved the light slowly, stepping in its bright puddle.

Every nerve quivered. He had decided. If the monster was there and chased him, he would run *away* from the girls. The light showed only rocks.

His soft-gripping shoes took him quietly to the ridge. He peered over, sliding the light across pink breathing bodies. He sighed with relief. Only babies. He went back up the slope. He was panting with tension. The stuffy atmosphere didn't help.

He found the pillar easily.

Lindsay wakened at his touch. Anaglypta snorted once, then was awake. Freddie pointed the torch at his own face. He mouthed the word string several times, until the others nodded. Their torches came on — fortunately, considering the tumble they'd taken — and they crept from the shelter of the pillar, probing the floor with ovals of light.

Lindsay's torch signalled. She lifted the ball of string from a groove in the rock and handed it to Freddie. They started to follow it, but stopped in dismay. Instead of leading them in a straight line, the string straggled everywhere, yards and yards of it, tangled and scattered over the floor of the cave.

Freddie saw the end and held it in the torchlight. The others gathered round. It was broken. The Enormouse must have snapped it and dragged it to the cave.

How were they going to get out?

Fear began to creep among Freddie's bones like a bug among twigs. Then it dissolved in a flood of astonishment, for Anaglypta did something neither Freddie nor Lindsay had ever seen her do before: she untied the bag of grub from her waist, tore open the plastic wrapper and handed out her sandwiches. She passed round the lemonade. There was a moment of stillness, just hands in the pool of light, Anaglypta's fat fingers pushing food to the others; then Lindsay was measuring how much lemonade they should drink – for it had to be rationed – and the grub disappeared into the darkness and three hungry mouths.

Freddie gathered in the string. He found a loop: the one he'd tied where they'd turned off the first tunnel. He hurried to the pillar dropping loose lengths behind him. He encircled the pillar and tied the string to it. He walked up the slope to the tunnel. Now they could return here if they had to, though he would rather go home. He would far, far rather go home.

He let Lindsay and Anaglypta go ahead, and Lindsay's light slid into the black hole of the tunnel. She stepped after it. Freddie payed out the string. The floor sloped up. Piles of giant mouse droppings threatened to trip them. Anaglypta gasped as tree roots touched her face. Freddie ducked under them. He was uneasy because the tunnel was levelling out – surely they had come downhill towards the cave? And it was an awful long way. They should have reached the junction by now. For many minutes the only sound had been the scuffing of their feet and the constant trickle of earth from the roof. He whispered, "We'll have to go back! We've come the wrong way!"

The girls turned. Lindsay's face was pale and her fair hair trembled as she nodded. Anaglypta's pink lip vibrated tearfully. Freddie didn't blame her. He didn't blame her at all.

They fumbled around and faced the way they'd come. Freddie's torch leapt on his wrist like a little wild animal as he wound furiously at the string. He bumped into Anaglypta and the string jumped away. He grabbed and missed. He clutched at his torch. He felt...

Oh, no!

Oh, not again!

The wind was pushing up the tunnel towards them!

"Run!" hissed Lindsay.

"The string!" gasped Freddie, but the wind tugged at his clothes and embraced him warmly, full of mousy smell. He couldn't have unwound the string fast enough anyway, so clutching Anaglypta's wrists, they fled into the unknown. Only the blobs of torchlight led them through unbelievable darkness, guided them round rocky corners, took them, plunging into new depths, staggering up earthen inclines. Then Lindsay stopped, and cried, "Oh!"

Before them was a wall.
A stone wall deep under the ground.
Blocking their way.
And behind them – the Enormouse!

9

"No!" cried Lindsay, and her torch danced wildly. "The tunnel follows the wall!"

And it did. Left, along the wall. Right, along the wall.

"Go left!" gasped Lindsay, and as Freddie hesitated and Anaglypta clung panting to his arm, Lindsay ripped open her bag of sandwiches and flung one sandwich a little way into the other tunnel. She threw a second one further, then frantically hurled the rest as far into the darkness as she could, then she pushed Freddie and Anaglypta into moving again and they raced on, lungs ripping with pain, heads aching in the stuffy, mousy air, wanting just to rest – to rest in safety.

The wind faded.

They collapsed in a heap, panting.

They heard an awful snuffling and grunting. The horrid animal noises grew muffled. "It's gone after the grub," said Lindsay. "But we must keep moving. Shift, Anaglypta, you're on my leg."

They walked quickly. Freddie was amazed at Anaglypta's lack of complaints.

"Look!" exclaimed Lindsay, and her torch moved across a pile of large square stones. The wall was at their right and in it was a solid black gap full of cool air. They crowded round and beamed the torches in. They saw more walls, some of brick, most of ancient stone. The floor was flagged with great squares of slate.

"It's the house!" said Freddie.

"The deep cellars!" said Lindsay.

"Come on!" they clambered over the tumbled blocks.

"Hold it!" said Freddie. He fumbled at his belt and pulled out...

"A dagger!" cried Lindsay. "Where did you get that?"

"Off one of the suits of armour. I know I maybe shouldn't have, but... We can mark our way so we don't get lost like that man ten years ago." And he scored an arrow on the nearest wall.

They moved slowly. A massive pillar loomed into the torchlight. They stood close to it. They held hands and stretched out but could scarcely reach quarter the way round. Close by, another pillar rose into the darkness. An arch joined the two. They moved the torches and saw more pillars dissolving beyond the light and archways towering into the gloom. They walked beneath them, like pygmies in a stone forest.

Freddie's arm ached with scraping.

"How could someone get lost for ever?" said Anaglypta, her voice echoing shrilly, "lost for ever ever ever..."

"Shssssh!" went echoing after Anaglypta's fading syllables.

"But how could they!" she whispered. "I know it's big, but it's only a house! Surely that man must have found the steps and door before he died of hunger! I want to sit down!"

"All right," agreed Lindsay. Their legs were jellified after running so hard, and Freddie guessed the girls felt safer under the house. He certainly did.

Maybe that was why Anaglypta was complaining again. Under real pressure she could take it, but now she felt safe...

She was right, though, about the man. How could he have got lost for ever? Freddie guessed *he* could walk round the house — outside — in fifteen or twenty minutes without hurrying. Surely, even in darkness, a man would stumble on the steps within a few hours, unless... Then he remembered why he was there with Lindsay and Anaglypta. Enormice. There were Enormice in the cellars!

"The mice got him," said Freddie.

"Shut up!" said Lindsay. "Let's move! One torch only. The batteries are fading."

They padded on across the giant flagstones, Lindsay's torch sliding eerily from pillar into darkness then to pillar, and stopping now and then for Freddie to scratch an arrow. "These are like church pillars," he remarked, but Lindsay said there was to be no more talking and they went on in silence, except for their scuffing feet and the occasional drip and click of things unexplained.

The light dimmed suddenly and darkness pressed around them. Then, when they could hardly see to the next pillar and Freddie's back was suffering the colly-wobbles, Lindsay pointed the light to one side and stopped.

They stared, and saw...

Steps!

The way out! The way to the white-walled cellar!

They hurried up the steps. They jostled. They panted. They clustered on the little landing.

Lindsay's torch flickered.

"There's no door!" she screamed.

Then the light went out.

10

"Switch on another torch!" said Lindsay frantically.

They fingered the wall where the door should have been. "It's bricked up!" gasped Freddie. Anaglypta sank on to the top step and heaved out a sob.

"But it's ancient!" whispered Lindsay. "Centuries old! Come on, Angalypta, it's the wrong door, that's all. We'll find the right one soon." And she patted Anaglypta's meaty shoulder.

They went down the steps, the stronger beam of the second torch showing dust and grit undisturbed perhaps since the house was built, until their clambering feet had come rushing up. They walked on. For hours, it seemed, hours and hours and hours, blackness pressing on their eyes and, once, Lindsay's steel nerves almost broke as she turned away from the arrow Freddie had cut and stepped into a giant cobweb which clung to her like a sticky blanket.

She shrieked and stood shuddering and whimpering as Freddie tore it from her and wiped her face with his sleeve and rubbed her hands with the front of his sweatshirt.

She didn't speak, but led on, the light trembling in her fingers.

They found a ladder. Freddie struck his shoulder against it in the darkness. They stared at the thick rungs, each piled with a delicate ridge of dust, each space curtained with cobwebs. Lindsay pointed the light up. The beam showed the ladder reaching as high as the pillar which supported it, and higher. It vanished into gloom above the arch. She gathered Freddie and Anaglypta close, and whispered so quietly they could scarcely hear. She said, "There's only one little door into the upper cellar and it's at the top of stone steps. This can't go anywhere."

"It's not the sort of ladder you move around," whispered Freddie. "It was built for a reason. It must go somewhere! We must try! I'm the lightest. I'll go first. It may not be safe." He borrowed his torch back from Lindsay and looped it to his wrist. "Mind the dust!" he hissed. Anaglypta's torch came on and the girls stepped back.

Hands through cobwebs; fingers breaking the ridges of dust from their centuries of sleep. Up he went. He wondered how Anaglypta would climb this. Probably she wouldn't have to. He stopped and sneezed as quietly as he could as the speckled air tickled his nose. He looked down. It was like peering over a stage in a theatre, with a little spotlight pointing up at him, tiny in the limitless blackness, its light spilling just enough to show the soft paleness of two weary faces.

The rung under him creaked. The four-teenth. He was glad he'd counted. He went carefully, gripping with his left hand, using the wrist of his right to hold each rung; in his fingers, the torch; on his sleeves, cobwebs. The arch curved near his face. He rested, panting dust. He climbed. The arch disappeared below him and his head went into darkness. He lifted the torch. Level with his chin was a floor. More flagstones. And another massive pillar. He swung the beam. More pillars! *Where was the white-walled cellar!*

He went down the ladder recklessly.

"It's not there!" he hissed. "It's not there!"

"What isn't?" demanded Lindsay.

"The ladder goes through the roof! The cellar isn't there! Just more pillars like this and another stone floor! *We're not under the house at all!*"

"Of course we are! Don't start snivelling, Anaglypta! And don't you, Freddie Faucet, be stupid! Where else could we be? There's no other building for miles except the house!"

"We ran miles!" sobbed Anaglypta.

"The nearest building is in the town and that's a forty minute drive away! We didn't run that far! We're under the house I tell you! Let me think. Put your torch off, Freddie."

"Maybe we're under the castle," he suggested, "in the old abbey."

"That's it! Of course!"

"We're under the castle?"

"No, no! How can all this be under the castle! It's part of the old abbey. Don't y'see? You said yourself it looked like a church! This is the abbey cellars – the crypt!"

"Oh!" moaned Anaglypta.

"The house cellars are on top!"

"But —"

"And the basement with the white walls is on top of *that*! And that explains why the door wasn't where we thought it would be. It's up above! C'mon!"

"Mind the fourteenth rung!" gasped Freddie.

Lindsay went up like an acrobat, then shone the torch down. Anaglypta climbed slowly but deliberately. Freddie stayed at her heels lighting the rungs, guiding her feet, hoping she wouldn't fall on him. Anaglypta was hauled safely on to the upper floor. Then they moved quickly, encouraged by the thought of finding the right steps, and the right door! The door to bright lights and fresh air! Freddie scored arrows, though there was little need, but he did it – just in case.

Once, something scrabbled in the darkness far among the stone columns. Lindsay's torch wouldn't reach and since it didn't bother them, they didn't bother it. But it set their hearts bumping.

Their hearts bumped more when Lindsay hesitated and said, "What's that?" in a husky whisper.

Something small and round, lay pale in the torchlight.

They went towards it cautiously, Anaglypta behind Freddie. Freddie switched his torch on it, and...

It looked up at him!

He drew in a breath. Lindsay squealed. And Anaglypta screeched, "It's the ghost!" and pulled vigorously at Freddie to make him run.

But the thing wasn't moving.

It simply looked.

"The shadows moved," said Freddie, "when I shone the torch. That didn't move. Look what it is." And he walked forward confidently and crouched down before Anaglypta's ghost.

"It's a skull!" gasped Lindsay.

"A skull?" whispered Anaglypta.

"It must be that man who was lost," said Freddie.

"But it jumped down on me!"

Freddie and Lindsay pointed the torches up and nearly fell over, for there in a niche above the arch gleamed many thin white lengths of...

"Bones!" cried Freddie.

"What was he doing up there!" exploded

Lindsay.

"Anaglypta must have disturbed him and his head fell off."

"Oh, don't," said Lindsay. "What was he *doing* up there?" She searched around with the torch then steadied it on the pillar the man had climbed. "It's all scratched!" she exclaimed.

"Clawmarks!" said Freddie.

"Enormice," said Lindsay.

"That's why he was lost for ever," gasped Anaglypta tearfully.

"Cheer up, Anaglypta," said Lindsay. She flashed her light along the roof. She went under the archway and giant shadows danced in silence. "Look!" came Lindsay's excited whisper. "The row of lights! The staircase is just along here!" And she dashed away.

Freddie and Anaglypta raced after her. Freddie smiled. Soon they'd be out of this dreadful place. They rushed up the steps. There was the steel door! At last! Push! Push!

Then they remembered.

Only then they remembered!

When they had left the cellars the last time, *they had bolted the door on the other side!*

11

"Oh, no!" Freddie sprawled with his back against the sill, tears hot in his eyes. That was the one thing they'd forgotten in their preparations!

Lindsay slid down beside him, head back and silent. Anaglypta stood sobbing.

They switched off one torch.

"What do we do now?" gulped Freddie.

"I want out!" said Anaglypta, and she turned and thumped the door with the lemonade bottle.

"Stop it!" snapped Lindsay. "It might be a month before anyone comes! There's only one thing we can do."

"What?" said Freddie dolefully. He didn't believe there was *anything* they could do.

"We go back."

"What!"

"I can't!" said Anaglypta. "Not all that way!"

"We don't know the way," said Freddie, "and the torches won't last."

"Listen," said Lindsay. "We ran miles when the Enormouse chased us — but just think how far we've really come..."

"What do you mean?"

"We've only come from the island to the house. You can walk that in five minutes. We must have run around these tunnels again and again. We were going in circles. I tell you we could be out again in a few minutes!"

"But we've been underground for hours!" wailed Anaglypta.

"We were feeling our way. We had to move quietly. We were taking minutes to travel a few yards."

"But the cave," said Freddie. "It was huge. There wasn't room for it under the lawn."

"We branched off, remember. It was a tunnel going to one side and down. *That* took us there. The cave must be under the wood. We could have gone straight on instead of down to the cave. Maybe that straight-on tunnel leads here! If we can find this end of it we can go directly to the island!"

"I'm not going!" cried Anaglypta, her voice echoing shrill in the darkness. "The lights are just through this door!"

"They might as well be on the moon!" snapped Lindsay. "We have to go back! There's no choice! There may be Enormice here. You either stay and get eaten or starve to death, or take a five minute walk into the sunshine! But first, we'll rest, then we'll eat. Then we'll go. No more talking."

So they rested.

Then they ate the last of the sandwiches.

Then, with the torches turning yellow, they walked down the stone steps, Lindsay clutching one torch and her camera; Freddie the dagger and the other torch; and Anaglypta the half-full bottle of lemonade. At their waists hung the straw bundles which, so far, had only been used as pillows, and in their pockets each of them carried a box of matches.

As Lindsay said, retracing their steps was easy. Freddie's arrows led them rapidly from one pillar to the next and, though the darkness was awful, their legs moved with new confidence.

Until they came to the ladder. A black square in the stone floor. Lindsay switched off her torch and Freddie lit the opening as she stepped into it backwards, feeling for the top rung. She began to go down. The top of her head gleamed fair in the yellow light. As she went down...

Oh!

As she went down...

Something began to come up!

12

Freddie saw the movement below her. He saw two wicked red dots as the thing reared bulkily on to the ladder.

"The Enormouse!" he yelled.

Lindsay hesitated. She didn't know if it was above or below.

"Come up!" screamed Freddie, for he saw teeth as big as the pages of a book. He grabbed Lindsay under the shoulder and pulled.

She gasped, and cried, "My foot!" and kicked wildly in terror, then she was up sprawling on the flagstones, yelling, "Light the straw! Light the straw! *Light the straw!*"

But Freddie didn't move. He was pointing the torch at a huge furry face and the shining eyes stared redly into the light. "The light's holding it!" he whispered. He heard a match strike and flames crackled on Lindsay's straw. It burned furiously billowing smoke and sparks into the darkness.

"Take that, you monster!" screamed Lindsay, and hurled the fire at the creature's face. There was a squeal and a scrabbling of claws. Then there was nothing below but cobwebs and the sparkling straw far beneath on the stone-flagged floor.

Freddie's heart hammered so hard he could

scarcely breathe. He remembered Lindsay's foot. "Did it bite you?" he panted.

"I don't know!" Lindsay's face was stony white. Her eyes were gigantic with fear. "You look," she whispered.

Freddie moved the light down her legs. Her denims were filthy with earth and cobwebs. Her right foot ... was OK. Her left foot...

He held the torch close. The heel and sole of her shoe dangled, attached only at the toe. He couldn't see any blood. He touched her foot; she didn't cry out. He moved her ankle; she said nothing.

He shone the torch on her face. Her eyes were shut.

"Is it still there?" she whispered.

"Yes. You're all right. But your shoe's no use."

Tears came reluctantly from under Lindsay's eyelids. "Turn that torch away!"

"I'll fix your shoe," said Freddie, and he untied Lindsay's lace and loosened enough of it to go under the sole. He pulled the sole into place and tied the lace firmly.

"It may do," he said.

"Let's go then!"

Anaglypta said nothing.

"Remember the creaky rung," said Freddie, and marvelled at this girl-cousin who was unhesitatingly stepping down into the world of the Enormouse.

144

Freddie went next, waiting for Anaglypta, guiding her feet.

They followed the torchlight among ancient pillars.

They pushed aside fantastic cobwebs.

They stared in astonishment at giant fungi growing like piles of dustbin lids in a damp corner.

And all the time Freddie had matches in his hand ready to light another straw torch, should the creature return.

They found the hole in the wall and clambered through.

"From here on," whispered Lindsay, "we're guessing, but if this is the wall of the house that faces the lake, all we have to do is keep our backs towards it – try to feel it's always behind us – and if we have to turn one way, make sure we turn the opposite way later. We can do it!" She pointed the torch at Anaglypta. Anaglypta's face was no longer round and full like the moon, but shrunken and worn and very dirty and very tear-stained. Cobwebs lay on her orange frizz like a hairnet. "Anaglypta," said Lindsay solemnly. "I didn't know you had it in you. You've been great. You too, Freckles," she added and turned away before either of them could speak.

They followed the wall, patting the great rough stones as they hurried along. They went carefully past the corner where Lindsay had thrown her sandwiches for the Enormouse. Her torch flickered. They waited anxiously as she tapped it. The light steadied and they sighed with relief. Then it went out.

The darkness rushed at them, suffocating, until Freddie split it with light. He pushed his torch into Lindsay's hand. No one spoke, but just one torch depressed them. They had matches and straw, but the straw gave more smoke than light and only lasted a minute or two. Freddie heard Anaglypta's breath shudder and he squeezed her fingers. It would be awful, lost in utter blackness!

"Freddie," whispered Lindsay, "put numbers on the wall."

"Why?"

"If we double back we'll have an idea how far we've come – arrows all look alike." She wiggled the dim torch significantly. "We can't waste any time."

Freddie dug a large 1 into the earthy wall. He counted ten paces and carved 2; then ten more; 3. He hoped this tunnel really would take them to the island. It was pretty straight. Then Lindsay groaned in a whisper as the light showed five black mouths waiting to swallow them. Five tunnels, and the torch fading by the minute!

Lindsay strode forward determinedly, choosing the most likely. Freddie cut numbers as quickly as his aching wrists would let him.

He wished the dagger was shorter and easier to use, but it was longer than a bread knife. Maybe it would be better just to hurry and not bother with numbers ... Then he remembered he had almost not bothered in the cellar. Sweat ran unpleasantly under his clothes at the thought. They'd never have found the ladder again if he hadn't. They burst into an open space.

Not the great cave where the babies slept, but a round cavern as high as a lamppost and wide enough to turn a car. In the softening glow of the torch, as Lindsay pointed the light up, the roof seemed stained with damp. Otherwise it was dry — though whether the thousand trickling noises were falling earth or dripping water Freddie couldn't tell. Many mouse droppings were trodden into the floor and scarred by clawmarks. Three new openings gaped at them.

"*None* of them feels right!" hissed Lindsay. She hurried to each in turn, with Freddie and Anaglypta as close as if they were tied to her elbows; she probed desperately with the fading light. "Which one?" she muttered, then to Freddie's surprise shone the torch in his face and her voice was a fearful whisper, "Which tunnel did we come out of?"

Freddie's mouth opened as he followed the torchlight round. Every tunnel was the same! What had he done? He started panting and sweating again. His legs trembled. The air was thick and warm.

"Calm down!" snapped Lindsay. "What was the last number?"

"Eighteen!" gasped Freddie.

"All we have to do is walk down each one until we find the number."

"Ten paces," said Freddie. "I put a number every ten paces."

"Come on!" she counted out loud and they crowded her heels, straining to find the scratched number, afraid of being left even a step behind in the awful blackness.

"Nothing! Turn round! Back!"

Freddie's ears felt funny, like when you go down a long hill in a bus. Air was pressing into them. A strong slow draught pushed at their clothes.

"It's coming!" gasped Lindsay, and they turned their backs to the cavern and the shifting air and fled quietly. The breeze faded. It's in the open space, thought Freddie. When the draught comes again it will be after us!

It came. Stronger. They ran in a curve. "We're at number 12!" panted Lindsay. "If we follow the numbers we'll be in the cavern again and maybe dodge the Enormouse! Oh! This shoe!" And she hopped several paces, then ran fiercely. "Just keep going!"

The walls receded and they were in the open space, huddled in the middle of its deep gloom, a thousand tricklings and dribblings sniggering around them. The wind swirled suddenly, filling the cavern with stench, and a vast roaring vibrated the walls. Earth showered their heads and Freddie felt water in his hair. The wind sighed like a giant and the sound of claws on rock mingled with terrifying bellows, and more earth fell in masses, smashing on to the floor, sending stones dancing and dust puffing in every direction.

Lindsay rushed towards a tunnel but squealed and fell over her torn shoe and the torch rolled, flickering miserably. Freddie snatched it up. Hurry, Lindsay! She got to her knees as another vast bellow shook the walls. A whole barrowful of earth plunged from above – and crushed Lindsay to the ground!

Freddie swung the torch. The Enormouse was beside them! Anaglypta screamed! Freddie stared in horror through the dim light. The monstrous mouse was bigger than he'd ever imagined! As big as an elephant, he'd thought. It could have torn an elephant to pieces!

Lindsay struggled in the loose earth. Freddie hauled at her and Anaglypta dug furiously, her fat arms moving like pistons.

"Lindsay!" screamed Freddie. He pointed the torch up at the Enormouse's face. Could he hypnotize it with the light like the one in the cellar? Or was the torch too dim? And this was a vastly bigger creature!

And it was turning towards them! The monster towered in the darkness, its eyes red rings as big as headlamps. Its unbelievable bulk almost filled the cavern. Lindsay was still trapped under the earth. She screamed, "Light the straw!" Anaglypta dug insanely. Freddie had forgotten about the straw. In his hand was the matchbox and loose matches he'd had ready since the last encounter. He knelt quickly and put the torch on the ground. He struck the bundle of matches furiously. *They didn't light!* They were wet with sweat from his hand! He dropped them and snatched more from the box.

"Freddie!"

He struck. The matches flared but went out as the Enormouse roared, sending down a blast of foul air.

He tried again. The matches lit. He rammed them into the straw. The straw fizzled hopelessly.

It was wet with spray from the roof!

Freddie screamed in horror. Anaglypta was a dim bulge in the darkness. The gigantic teeth were descending!

It was going to eat Lindsay and there was nothing any of them could do!

13

Two things happened.

Anaglypta waved her arms as if shooing away a dog; Lindsay used the camera. It was looped to her wrist and she pointed it up. The flash flooded the place with stunning white light. For an instant, Freddie saw every hair on the Enormouse's body. He saw the eyes, round and brilliant, shrink from the light and the gigantic ears turn in fear. Every stone and earthy crumb of the cavern was outlined in shadow. The beast hesitated blindly and Freddie's glance went to Anaglypta's waving arms and he saw, glittering, half buried in the earth, the lemonade bottle.

The bottle.

Freddie lunged and grabbed it. He swung it vigorously. Earth spattered all around. Lemonade fizzed angrily. Lindsay was up!

"Run!" gasped Freddie, and the bottle slipped. It fled from his fingers in the wrong direction! It would miss the Enormouse! The jaws gaped! The bottle flew past the jaws, heading for the wall!

The bottle exploded like a bomb.

Earth burst from the roof and plunged among them, crashes mingling with the roars of the great mouse. Dust spumed everywhere. Freddie screamed for Lindsay and Anaglypta as they vanished into the thickening air. The torch in his hand was a pale blob dancing insanely. Something grabbed his arm.

"Run!" howled Lindsay. "Anaglypta's here!"

The noise increased. Water struck Freddie's shoulder, wetting him down to his shoes. "It's collapsing!" he yelled. "Run! Run!" And they fled, straight into the nearest tunnel. Lindsay fell, swearing at her shoe. Freddie hoisted her and pushed her ahead, and even in that frantic second couldn't help admiring her, for Lindsay grabbed Anaglypta with one hand and fired the flash of the camera with the other to light the way. Lindsay was always thinking! Freddie saw something in the brilliant light. He threw himself on his knees. It was the string! They were in the right tunnel!

"We're in the right one!" he gasped, but nobody heard. Lindsay and Anaglypta were gone, and something knocked Freddie's ankles from under him. He sprawled forward, earth spattering his head and back, and, oh horror! across his hands slithered an awful dark thing, scaly and long, dragging dustily in the puddle of torch light.

And the Enormouse roared beside him! He rolled over clutching at a pain in his ribs, and found in his grasp the dagger! He'd thrust it into his belt!

The gargantuan body of the Enormouse

pressed him against the wall. The beast hadn't seen him but it would catch Lindsay and Anaglypta.

Freddie stabbed wildly. Again and again he thrust deep into the grey-brown fur; again and again he dug the blade deep, and his own screams mingled with the moans of his fantastic enemy.

He went on stabbing until his arms were numb. He wondered why the Enormouse hadn't attacked him. Of course! It couldn't turn in the tunnel! It bellowed and buffeted Freddie, thudding him in its agony against the wall. If its fur hadn't been so thick, he would have been squashed flat a hundred times. Dust filled his eyes, nostrils and mouth.

Suddenly, the Enormouse was gone. The air was a yellow fog. Freddie splashed through water. Had the girls escaped? It couldn't be far to the hole inside the castle. Was the Enormouse ahead?

He walked into the wall. He didn't see it for dust. But he hadn't time to be astonished. Yelling and screaming came from above.

"The rope's in front of you!" howled Lindsay. "Climb!" And the rope leapt, striking his face as someone jerked it.

He climbed up the knots for a thousand years. Then he fell out into daylight, and the girls were there, pulling him to his feet. He was blinded by the evening sun.

"You shouldn't still be here!" he gasped.

"You're crazy!" yelled Lindsay.

Dust belched from the pit and terrible roars came from inside the earth. "It's coming!"

"I can't run!" said Freddie.

"He's covered in blood!" screamed Anaglypta. "Blood and dust!"

"It's not mine!" Freddie almost fell. He felt as if he'd been trampled by a hundred elephants.

Then he was dragged through shrubs and trees and across the grassy bank. He could see now and he stared in horror.

"The boat!" he whispered. Only the prow was showing. The rest was not only under water — it was under a great pile of stones. The castle wall had fallen on it.

14

More stones tumbled over the grass and splashed into the lake. The roar of the Enormouse blasted across the countryside. Behind the collapsing walls, moved the great bulk, brown with dirt.

"It's out!" gasped Lindsay. They stared in terror. The Enormouse was free and the boat lay splintered at the bottom of the lake!

For once, Anaglypta was quicker than Lindsay. "We'll swim," she said, and strode into the water. Lindsay flung herself after her and Freddie followed.

He was so tired. He swam deep, weeds trailing his face, the cool and cleansing pressure washing around him. Something above broke the surface and fell massively past in a buzzing cloud of bubbles. A thousand claws tore at his clothes, turning him over. It was only a tree, but he spun and didn't know which way was up. And he didn't care. He was too tired to hold his breath. A dozen thin limbs held him within the water's fresh embrace...

His hair was being pulled out by the roots. He was rushing along and his head burst into sunlight. He gasped frantically. Whatever gripped his hair twisted painfully, forcing him over on his back; then little fingers cupped his chin and he was floating, sculling gently through the water, facing the island. Stones rolled everywhere. The Enormouse in its pain was dashing against the castle walls, rushing among trees. An oak, more ancient, probably, than the castle, and immensely strong, snapped as the Enormouse blundered against it. The creature turned. On its side a patch of dust hung thick and sticky and Freddie thought he could see the handle of the dagger.

His heels dragged on mud. Anaglypta helped him sit up and Lindsay, white faced and dripping, gaped in horrified astonishment. "What's happening to the lake?" she whispered.

Water bubbled and burped. Tips of plants broke the surface. Fish leaped in panic. Patches of mud rose glistening into the sunlight.

"It's running out," said Freddie. "Down into the tunnels."

They sat, exhausted, aching to their bones. Even when the Enormouse rushed down the island's shore and floundered towards them they couldn't find strength to move. And when a vast spurt of dust exploded from the castle with a WHUMP! they scarcely jumped. And the Enormouse thrashed through the lake. But it was clumsy. The great animal crouched suddenly, trembling, the fur of its chest and sides washed clean. A red stain spread into the water. The Enormouse roared pitifully.

Freddie was aware of people gathering on the lawn and he heard the thin screams of peacocks far away in the gardens, but he paid no attention. He wanted to cry. The Enormouse staggered towards them, then knelt, a river of blood pumping into the lake. It shuddered, and its head rolled to one side.

All round, the lake drained noisily away, leaving mud, folded weeds and hundreds of gasping fish.

"He's dead," said Freddie.

15

They had stood, rather stunned, on the balcony of Lindsay's suite and watched Alec directing the work. Boards and catwalks were laid on the mud. Fish were rescued, swimming in buckets and basins, troughs and plastic bags – anything that would hold water. Straw bales were rushed over the catwalks and packed around the Enormouse to prevent it sinking deeper. Photographs were taken, some of Freddie, Lindsay and Anaglypta, a few of Alec and Alexandra, hundreds of the Enormouse.

Things quietened. The sun was a red ball among the trees, gazing through the dust that still hung above the castle. Spotlights glimmered on round the great beast and someone walked on the straw bales, keeping guard. Bangs and groans drifted occasionally, muffled, from deep under the lawn.

"The lake," said Freddie, "will have filled the cave where the babies slept."

They had said almost nothing. What they felt couldn't be turned into words. The Enormouse was dead. They couldn't believe it. It was just too big, too powerful, and now ... so motionless, with the sun dipping beyond the countryside, leaving the mud dark and red, and the spotlights brightening, illuminating the tremendous ears, the closed eyes.

Then they had baths; and Freddie's spirits lifted when Alec took him to Lindsay's room, trudging through in his slippers and dressing gown. Anaglypta was there and a special supper prepared by Alexandra.

They ate, and talked suddenly, and crowded at Lindsay's dressing-table mirror to compare scrapes and bruises; then everyone was quiet when Freddie spoke about the Enormouse buffeting him against the tunnel wall, and the dagger... He almost wished he hadn't taken the dagger.

And Lindsay kept saying how terrific he'd been, and Alec and Alexandra gazed in mild astonishment at Anaglypta on hearing how pluckily she'd behaved all through the amazing adventure and how her quick thinking had got them off the island, while Freddie and Lindsay were still shocked by the loss of the boat; and they positively gaped as if seeing Anaglypta for the first time when Lindsay told them she'd saved Freddie from drowning by her knowledge of life-saving. There was no doubt, thought Freddie, Anaglypta *was* different. The permanent scowl had cleared from her face and he would have bet almost anything that Anaglypta had blubbed her last blub.

Lindsay had crawled into bed. Alec was talking about opening the tunnels to the public. "In other words," grinned Lindsay, her eyes half closed, "you'll make a fortune!"

"That's the idea," said Alec. "The universities will give their back teeth for a look at that thing. There may even be a live one in the cellar! And the photographs you took of the babies will be published in every newspaper in the world... I say! Anaglypta's stopped eating. She's asleep. So is Lindsay. Slide down, old thing, under the covers. Take Anaglypta to her room, will you, Alexandra? I'll see to Freddie. Little blighter's out for the count."

And, for a moment, Freddie thought he was on a bus leaving behind everything he knew, then he realized that the arms that lifted him and laid him in his bed were arms that loved him.

A faint cigar smell came close and a bristly kiss touched his forehead.

"Goodnight, old son," said Alec.

"Goodnight, Dad," sighed Freddie. "See you in the morning."